MURDER SWEETLY SERVED

COCOA NAREL CHOCOLATE SHOP MYSTERIES
BOOK 1

MORGANA BEST

BEST Cozy Books

Murder Sweetly Served

Cocoa Narel Chocolate Shop Mysteries, Book 3

Print ISBN 978-1-925674-02-6

By this act
And words of rhyme
Trouble not
These books of mine
With these words I now thee render
Candle burn and bad return
3 times stronger to its sender.
(Ancient Celtic)

GLOSSARY

NOTE FROM THE AUTHOR

I have used Australian spelling in this series, so for example, *Mum* instead of the US spelling *Mom, neighbour* instead of the US spelling *neighbor, realise* instead of the US spelling *realise*. It is *Ms, Mr* and *Mrs* in Australia, not *Ms., Mr.* and *Mrs.; cosy* and not *cozy; 1930s* not *1930's; offence* not *offense; centre* not *center; towards* not *toward; jewellery* not *jewelry; favour* not *favor; mould* not *mold; two storey house* not *two story house; practise* (verb) not *practice* (verb); *odour* not *odor; smelt* not *smelled; travelling* not *traveling; liquorice* not *licorice; lent* not *leaned; have concussion* not *have a concussion; anti clockwise* not *counterclockwise; go to hospital* not *go to the hospital; sceptic* not *skeptic; aluminium* not *aluminum; learnt* not *learned*. These are just some of the differences.

Please note that these are not mistakes or typos, but correct Aussie spelling and terms.

AUSTRALIAN SLANG AND TERMS

Big Smoke - a city

Blighter - infuriating or good-for-nothing person

Blimey - an expression of surprise

Blue - an argument

Bluestone - copper sulphate (copper sulfate in US spelling)

Bluo - a blue laundry additive, an optical brightener

Bogan - someone considered to be rough, low-life, "trailer-trash"

Boot (car) - trunk (car)

Bonnet (car) - hood (car)

Bunging it on - faking something, pretending

Cark it - die

Come good - turn out okay

Copper, cop - police officer

Coot - silly or annoying person

Crikey! - an expression of surprise

Drongo - an idiot

Fair crack of the whip - a request to be fair, reasonable, just

Flat out like a lizard drinking water - very busy

Galah - an idiot

Garbage - trash

G'day - Hello

Give a lift (to someone) - give a ride (to someone)

Goosebumps - goose pimples

Laundry (referring to the room) - laundry room

Like a stunned mullet - very surprised

Mad as a cut snake - either insane or very angry

Miles - while Australians have kilometres these days, it

is common to use expressions such as, "The road stretched for miles," "It was miles away."

Mow (grass / lawn) - cut (grass / lawn)

Swag - a (temporary) bedroll

Stone the crows! - an expression of surprise

Takeaway (food) - Take Out (food)

Torch - flashlight

Tuck in (to food) - to eat food hungrily

Ute /Utility - pickup truck

Vegemite - Australian food spread, thick, dark brown

Wardrobe - closet

Indigenous References

Bush tucker - food that occurs in the Australian bush

Koori - the original inhabitants/traditional custodians of the land of Australia in the part of NSW in which this book is set. *Murri* are the people just to the north. White European culture often uses the term, *Aboriginal people.*

CHAPTER 1

"But Carl, it's not my birthday."

Carl leant across to me and put his finger to his lips. "Shush, he'll hear you. Besides, I know it's not your birthday. It's just a figure of speech."

I peeped around the kitchen door, but the man was not yet harmed. That in itself was a plus. I turned back to Carl. "I'm not sure I get your meaning."

Carl smirked at me. "I mean, when I said birthday present, I just wanted to give you a gift."

I held up my hands in exasperation. "But *Catman*?"

Carl made a snort of disgust. "His name isn't Catman, Narel! His name is *The Purr-suader*. Peter Patterson is a Cat Whisperer, a very famous Cat Whisperer. He's a five times USA Today Times bestselling author and he has that documentary series, *The Purr-suader World*."

"Yes, he told me at least five times." I peeped around the door once more. "Are you sure he won't sue us, after, well you know…" My voice trailed away.

Carl gave me a playful slap on the arm. "Narel, have

some confidence in the man. Haven't you seen his show?" Without waiting for me to answer, he pushed on. "If anyone can solve Mongrel's aggression problems, he can."

"But the guy just turned up on my doorstep last week. Do famous Cat Whisperers go door to door, and in small country towns at that?"

Carl frowned. "This one obviously does! And if I hadn't been here at the time, you would've turned him away. The Purr-suader will turn Mongrel into a sociable, well-behaved cat in no time at all."

I thought it was too good to be true, but I also thought I should attempt a positive attitude. "Okay then. Should we offer him lunch first?" I opened my second fridge, the one where I kept the commercial chocolates, and looked inside, but I heard a deep male voice behind me, and spun around.

"Mongrel and I have made firm friends already," Peter The Purr-suader announced in a calm, assertive manner.

I eyed the man warily. Weren't people supposed to look like their pets? He didn't look anything like a cat—a goat, maybe. He had a short beard that was desperately in need of a beard trimmer, and his wild mane of grey-blond hair stuck out at all angles. His jeans were bright green, a fact I found rather strange, and his shirt was lime green. All in all, it was not a good look, unless you were a leprechaun. "But Mongrel hasn't come out of his carrier basket yet," I said, bewildered.

"I don't encourage cats to leave their baskets before they're ready," he explained in an overly condescending tone, "and please keep your tone low and calm. Mongrel and I have made eye contact, and he now knows that I'm the Cat Leader. I can assure you that cat aggression problems are an even more common issue than litterbox problems. Now, there is no such thing as a born aggressive cat—it's always the human who has caused the aggression in the cat." He fixed me with an accusing glare.

"I got him like that," I said defensively.

"They all say that." He snorted rudely, but then smiled a thin-lipped smile. "May I ask why you have a refrigerator full of chocolates?"

I didn't know what that had to do with anything, but answered nonetheless. "I own the Cocoa Narel Chocolate Shop, and tonight I'm providing special chocolates for an office retirement party."

Peter clapped his hands in delight. "May I see?"

I opened the fridge door again. "Those are chocolate red Porsches, to match the client's car," I said, pointing to the contents, "and those are little chocolate road bikes. I've also done a variety of other chocolates, such as football shoes and boots, and animals, like the chocolate koalas, kangaroos, crocodiles, and snakes." I gestured expansively, and then took out a little box. I placed it on the table and then shut the fridge door.

"Look, but don't touch," I cautioned him. "These are a special request for the client. These are…"

He interrupted me. "Toadstools."

I held up the box so he could get a better look. "Fly agaric, to be precise. The toadstools of fairytales, red with white spots. The bases are meringue, and the tops are chocolate and marzipan. I handmade all these."

"All of them?" Peter looked impressed.

"Yes."

"And the mushrooms are just for the client?"

I nodded. "Yes, they're a special gift. The other chocolates are for all the guests."

Peter appeared to have lost interest. "I have some wonderful flower essential oil essences out there that will help Mongrel become calm."

I placed the chocolates back in the fridge, and Carl and I followed Peter back into the living room. Carl headed straight for an open box of little bottles on the coffee table. He at once had his hands in the box and selected a bottle. He opened it and dabbed some behind his ears. "Ylang Ylang, one of my favourites!"

The Purr-suader selected another bottle. "Lavender is often a suitable calming cat essential oil, but I'll offer Mongrel a selection."

I clutched Carl in fear as Peter approached Mongrel's open basket. He held a bottle of essential oil at the door of the basket, and to my surprise, Mongrel stuck his head out and sniffed it. "Wow, that's amazing!" I exclaimed. "I thought Mongrel would attack you."

Peter turned to me. "I know what I'm doing, my dear. I'm an expert, after all. It's usual for a cat to hunt and kill. That's simply normal predatory aggression. It becomes a problem when people play rough with their cats, because this type of behaviour is then encouraged."

"Trust me, I didn't play rough with Mongrel," I said.

Peter narrowed his eyes. "That is beside the point. From what you have told me, Mongrel's behaviour is either redirected aggression or fear-induced aggression. It seems clear he has a bad association with rope."

"Yes, Carl bought him from an animal shelter for me. The shelter people said that the farmer treated him cruelly and used to tie him up with rope. Now he goes crazy whenever he sees rope. Isn't that right, Carl?"

Carl nodded furiously.

I would have said more, but Peter held up his hand to stop me speaking. "No matter, that's all in the past. Animals don't retain memories in the same way that people do. I'll offer Mongrel some more essential oils, and when I find the one he likes, I will dab some on the outside of his basket. When he's suitably calm, I will start extinction therapy."

I certainly didn't share his view that animals didn't remember in the same way in which humans did, but now I was really worried. "Extinction therapy?" I squeaked. "Isn't that like where you put someone who is terrified of spiders in a room with hundreds of spiders?" I clutched myself and shuddered.

Peter frowned. "Nothing quite so dramatic. I will start in a very small way. As Mongrel doesn't like ropes, I need to make seeing a rope a pleasant experience for him. For example, I'll talk in soothing tones and put the essential oil on his basket. Then I will place a small piece of rope in a bowl of cat food, and that will be enough for the first day."

I wasn't so sure.

Peter was still talking. "My aim is to get Mongrel to associate ropes with a pleasant experience, rather than the fears of his past."

"It sounds good in theory, I suppose," I said, and would have said more, but Peter was already busily dabbing essential oil on Mongrel's basket. Mongrel still hadn't left his basket, which showed me that he wasn't too sure of

Peter, but then again, he wasn't usually good with strangers.

"Narel, would you get some of Mongrel's cat food?"

I did as I was asked, and soon returned with Mongrel's favourite dry cat food. Peter poured some into a little dish and then put a tiny piece of rope in the dish. I eyed it warily, but then decided it was too small to make Mongrel react. Nevertheless, Carl and I backed away to a corner of the room.

Peter looked at me. "May I fetch myself a glass of water first, to calm my aura?"

I nodded. "Sure. I'll just get it for you."

"I'll do it." Peter disappeared into the kitchen.

When he returned, apparently hydrated, he placed the bowl in front of Mongrel's basket just far enough away that Mongrel had to leave his basket to get the food. At first, the basket shook violently, and then Mongrel ran out. He devoured every morsel of dry food greedily, turned around, and ran back into his basket, all in double quick time. I was relieved that he hadn't seemed to notice, or even eaten, the tiny piece of rope, so I was surprised that Peter had gone white.

"What's wrong, Peter?" I asked him. "I thought that went rather well, didn't it?"

Carl agreed.

"Err, um, I've never seen a cat like that before," Peter said. "What happened to his ear?"

I shrugged. "No idea. He came like that, with one ear crooked and bent over."

Peter was still trembling. "He moves fast, doesn't he! He seems a little, um, more aggressive than I thought."

"But we explained how aggressive he was the other day," Carl said, sounding rather put out.

Peter made a gesture of dismissal. "I thought you were exaggerating. People always exaggerate when they explain their cat's behaviour."

Carl and I exchanged glances. "Well, I can understand if you don't want to work with Mongrel anymore," I said.

Carl glowered at me. "But it's my gift to you, Narel."

Peter placed the bottles of essential oils in his basket. "It's fine; it's fine. There's no cat I can't handle. See, he didn't even react to the rope. I'll need to start this extinction therapy with a slightly bigger piece of rope."

"If you're sure that's a good idea," I said. "You saw what he was like just then, and that's him in a good mood."

"Look, I'm The Purr-suader," Peter said firmly, fixing me with a withering look. "I'm the expert here." Before Carl or I could stop him, he reached into his box and pulled out a small piece of rope.

~

After the ambulance had collected Peter, Carl and I sat down over a cup of hot chocolate and some strawberry soft-centred chocolates to recover from our ordeal.

I set down my cup. "That was probably what saved him—the fact that it was a tiny length of rope."

Carl shook his head sadly. "I'm sorry it didn't turn out to be such a good gift, after all."

I shrugged. "It was a lovely thought, and Mongrel looks happy."

Mongrel was watching us, sitting on the chair at the end of the kitchen table, his two ginger paws resting on the table. I didn't particularly want cat paws on the table, but I certainly wasn't brave enough to object.

"I'm sure he's improving," Carl said, although not very convincingly. He let out a long sigh. "Do you need me to help you get ready for the office retirement party tonight?"

I shook my head. "Everything's under control, but thanks for the offer. I'm a bit shaken though, to be honest, after what happened to The Purr-suader. I don't know how I'm going to pull myself together and serve all the chocolates tonight."

Carl swallowed a chocolate before answering. "It will be a piece of cake. After all, I'll be there to help you, and the day could hardly get any worse, now could it?"

CHAPTER 2

"This is a little too fancy," Carl said.

I eyed him suspiciously. I thought he was being overly sarcastic, but then again, you never knew with Carl. "You're joking, right?"

Carl snorted with disgust. "Of course I am. Still, I like the scented candles."

I surveyed the large room before me. It was cold, grey, and clinical, with bright fluorescent lights. All in all, it was a typical office room, in this case, a conference room converted to a party room. Someone had attempted to add a party atmosphere by placing balloons and scented candles around the room, and even some lucky bamboo, although I wasn't sure of the reason for that. Soft music played in the background, but all in all, nothing could change the fact that it was a conference room, and so the scented candles stood out as incongruous.

"I wonder why they couldn't have afforded a nice room in town, maybe at a restaurant," Carl said.

I elbowed him in the ribs. "Shush. Someone might hear you."

Carl ignored me. "There's no one here yet. Maybe they couldn't afford a restaurant after paying you for catering."

"I hardly catered this event, Carl," I said, somewhat put out. "I only catered the chocolates for the event. I run a chocolate shop, not a catering firm, if you hadn't noticed."

Carl was still off in his own world. "The Purr-suader would love all these scented candles. This room would certainly calm down a lot of cats."

I laughed. "Yes, but only if the candles were all lavender scented. I think they've chosen every variety of fragrant candles at random, and just stuck them around the room. I think it would have been a better effect if they had just selected one scent."

Carl sneezed. "Yes, I have to agree with you. Now what do we do?"

"Miriam Moreton, the organising lady, told me to put all the chocolates on this table under the window." I gestured to an empty table by the window. It had a starched white tablecloth over it that wouldn't have looked out of place in a hospital.

Carl rolled his eyes. "I'm not an event organiser, but even *I* could have done a better job. They should have hired me to run this function, but it's clear they didn't hire anyone."

I simply shrugged, and before long, the two of us were busy arranging the chocolates on the table. I now owned a small chocolate fountain, because I had recently been asked to provide chocolates for events such as these, and it had proven cheaper to buy one rather than hiring it as I had in the past. "Carl, I think we should place the chocolate animals here, and those triple chocolate fudge brownie chocolates there."

"Where should we place the fly agaric chocolates?"

I gestured to the centre of the table. "There for now, but I'll check with Miriam."

"Should we leave them in the box?"

I nodded. "Yes. I don't know if Miriam wants to present them in the box, so that's why I left them in the gift box."

I had spoken to Miriam, the organiser who was also Stan's personal secretary, earlier, but there had been no sign of her the whole time we were setting up the chocolates. She now bustled into the room, a picture of efficiency. "That looks lovely, Narel. Your chocolates are delightful." I could see she wanted to eat one, maybe a whole bunch. And who could blame her?

"Thank you. I left the chocolates that are especially for Mr Wellings in that gift box. Would you like me to take off the lid and display them or leave them in the box?"

"In the box for now," she said. "I don't want anyone else to eat them by mistake until I present them to him. Should we place some candles on the table with the chocolates?"

"Candles will make the chocolates melt," Carl said, clearly aghast.

Miriam looked doubtful. "I suppose you're right. I didn't mean to place them close to the chocolates. It's just that this room is so impersonal." She cast a glance around the empty room before continuing. "Normally, we would have a retirement party at the local restaurant, only well, Stan Wellings isn't well liked." Her voice trailed away, and her cheeks flushed red, as if she had just disclosed a dreadful secret.

"I suppose there's a lot of competition in an advertising agency," Carl said.

Miriam nodded vigorously. "Yes, there is. Although this is a small country town, our office does a lot of business in the capital cities. It's a short flight from here to Sydney and Brisbane, and the flight to Melbourne isn't even that long. Of course, with the internet these days, the running costs of an office are much cheaper in the country and we always fly to the clients."

She continued to talk about advertising agencies in suitable locations, but my mind drifted back to the chocolates. I had to admit, it was an impressive array, and I was pleased that my hard work had paid off.

I jumped when I realised that Miriam was addressing me directly. "Sorry?"

Miriam looked at her watch. "I said that people will be starting to arrive, so would you turn on the chocolate fountain now?"

"Sure." I set myself to filling the fountain with just the right amount of chocolate.

Carl and I had to stay throughout the event, as I had to monitor the chocolate fountain. I had to make sure I added more chocolate from time to time, as the chocolate was consumed. I would rather have been at home watching the latest series of *The Bachelorette*, but Carl was happy to stay with me. He was something of a social butterfly. Thinking of *The Bachelorette* reminded me that I hadn't heard from my crush, Borage, lately.

"Have you heard from Porridge lately?" Carl asked me.

I shook my head. "Carl, sometimes I think you're

psychic. I was just thinking about Borage. And stop calling him Porridge—you know how much that annoys me."

Carl laughed. "Yes, and that's exactly why I do it."

"If you tease me about Borage, I'll start teasing you about Detective Rieker."

That had the desired effect. Carl's face flushed various shades of red. Carl had something of a crush on Detective Rieker, although he wouldn't admit to it. Since I had moved back to town, there had been several murders, and unfortunately, I had discovered some of the bodies. That was how I had met the obnoxious-but-just-doing-his-job Detective Clyde and the attractive-to-Carl Detective Rieker. At any rate, there was no time to ponder such events, because the guests were starting to arrive.

I didn't know any of them, and I feared this evening might be boring, or uncomfortable, to say the least. Various well dressed but bored-looking people filed into the room, some with partners, some alone. I recognised Stan Wellings when he walked into the room, because everybody clapped. At his side was a tall, slender woman. I guessed her young enough to be his daughter, granddaughter even. Despite her youth, she'd had so much plastic surgery that her face looked wildly distorted. I wondered why someone so young would have felt the need to resort to such measures, and I said this to Carl in a whisper.

"Maybe she's ninety," Carl said. "Maybe she's not young after all."

I wasn't so sure. She had an impossible figure, huge lips, a highly stretched face, and a tiny waist. She giggled incessantly.

A man appeared at my side and held out his hand. I shook it automatically. "I'm Craig Cooper," he said. "I haven't seen the two of you around here before."

"I'm Narel Myers, and this is my friend, Carl Camden," I said. "I own the *Cocoa Narel Designer Chocolate Shop*. I catered the chocolates for tonight."

Craig's eyes widened. "You're Cocoa Narel! I've heard all about you."

I didn't know if that was a good thing. Carl and I exchanged glances.

"You were the one who had the terrible car accident, weren't you? And you had loads of plastic surgery because you were so badly injured in the accident, and you came back to town many months later, looking quite different." If Craig noticed my discomfort, he certainly showed no sign. "And when you were young, you couldn't stop eating chocolate which was why you looked like you did, and now you can't put on any weight." He chuckled. "And now you can eat as much chocolate as you like and not put on weight, after all your surgeries."

"That's right," I said through clenched teeth.

"You're quite famous around here," the tactless Craig continued. "Weren't some of your classmates murdered right after you came back to town?"

I simply glared at him, but he pushed on. "Yes, that's right. I remember it all now. You were a suspect, weren't you! The victims were the ones who'd bullied you horribly at school, and they died one by one. The police thought it was you."

Carl finally spoke up. "Narel wasn't the only one they bullied."

The man nodded. "Quite so, quite so. Anyway, I'm sure

they got what was coming to them." He looked pointedly at Stan Wellings. "Now that's someone who has managed to avoid getting what's coming to him, so far. With any luck the karma train will get him sooner or later."

I was relieved that he had changed the subject. "The two of you don't get along? I've heard Mr Wellings isn't popular."

Craig made a choking sound. "That's the understatement of the century. The only person who likes him is that bimbo, Peaches." He held up his hands. "I'm not kidding—that's her name, Peaches. Can you believe it? She's a complete airhead, a total bimbo. I think she's younger than his daughter." He nodded to an elegant young woman on the far side of the room. "That's Minnie. She was dating a local sheep shearer, but Stan said he wasn't good enough for her and he forced them to break up. I'm surprised she still speaks to her father after that."

"Is Stan's ex-wife still in town?" I asked him.

"No, she died some years ago. Minnie's the only child. Of course, Stan's been having affairs ever since his wife died, and no doubt he was before that, too. I'm sure Peaches is only after him for his money."

"Do advertising executives make a lot of money?" Carl asked with obvious interest.

Craig shrugged. "It depends. Stan has no scruples, so he'll stop at nothing to get what he wants. He made some big deals in Sydney and could've retired on the money, but he said he'd be too bored. That's why he came to this agency out here in the country. He's a very wealthy man so he doesn't need to work, hence Peaches the girlfriend. She's a little gold digger, that one. Oh, speaking of gold diggers! Crikey! There's that bogan, Mick Holder. Don't look now."

Of course, the first thing I did was look. The man who just walked through the door was wearing a flannelette shirt and jeans. He also seemed to be wearing steel-capped boots. Sure, it wasn't party gear, but I didn't understand why Craig had such a strong reaction.

Craig kept talking. "Minnie must've invited him to cause trouble. There's going to be one huge scene when Stan spots him. Well, if you'll excuse me, I'll help myself to a drink and get ready for the show."

"I didn't think this party was going to end up being so exciting," Carl said. "Mind you, it isn't exciting yet, but it sounds like it could be soon."

I shrugged. "Mick is hiding behind people, and not going up to Minnie, so he's not trying to irritate Stan by the looks of it. Anyway, who knows? Let's get ourselves a drink."

Carl agreed. "I was waiting for a waiter to walk past and offer me a glass of champagne from a silver tray, but that clearly isn't going to happen here. Your chocolates are the best thing about this party, Narel."

I had to agree. "I wonder why they paid for my chocolates. I mean, you would think they would just go to the local supermarket and buy any old chocolates, given the look of the wine."

Carl laughed. "What, you're not partial to Passion Pop?" He pointed to a label on a wine bottle and then placed it down. "Well, here's a bottle of cheap Moscato. It's sparkling."

I held out my plastic champagne glass, and Carl filled

it. "Narel, I think I'm going to die of boredom, simply die of boredom."

Just then, a middle-aged woman burst into the room. The first thing I noticed was that she wasn't dressed for the party, and appeared to be dressed in everyday household clothes. In fact, she was wearing an apron.

She marched straight over to Stan, who hadn't noticed her arrival, as he was standing with his back to her. She grabbed his arm and spun him around. Even from where I was standing, I could see that all the colour drained from his face. He took a step backwards into Peaches, who put her arm around him to steady him.

"You cheated on me!" the woman screamed at the top of her lungs. She stabbed him in the chest with her stubby finger. "You cheated on me, with that whore."

CHAPTER 3

The apron-wearing woman pointed to Peaches. "I can't believe it! I just can't believe it!" she screamed, now pummelling Stan's chest with her hands. "You said you worked late hours, and you'd never take me to parties, and I thought you were just busy, but now I find out the truth! You've been playing me all along! You were never going to marry me!"

I realised I was standing there with my mouth open, and shut it. "That poor woman," I whispered to Carl.

"Shouldn't someone do something?" he whispered back.

I did think it was strange that no one came to Stan's aid, but then again, Miriam had said he was unpopular.

"Someone call the police!" Stan said. "Can't you see the woman's assaulting me?"

The woman drew back her leg and kicked Stan in the shins. He doubled over with a screech of pain. Miriam and Craig went straight to the woman and tried to calm her. She was now screaming obscenities at Stan. With some difficulty, Craig, Miriam, and two men I didn't know managed to get the woman out of the room.

Peaches stood there with her hand over her mouth. I figured she was wondering whether she should go to Stan's aid, or berate him for two-timing her. It appeared she was having trouble deciding, because she continued to stand, frozen in the same position, while Minnie took her father by the arm and led him over to a chair by the chocolate table.

Miriam and Craig presently returned to the room. Carl hurried over to Miriam, and I followed him. "Is everything all right?" Carl asked her.

Miriam shook her head. "An unpleasant business. That's Daphne Delamare, Stan's live-in housekeeper." She shook her head. "An unpleasant business," she said again. "Oh dear!"

"What's wrong?" I asked her.

Miriam nodded in Stan's direction. "Minnie has just offered him that box of chocolates. You know, the ones I was going to present him as a special gift later."

I tried to comfort her. "Well, he's had a terrible shock," I said, doing my best to sound sympathetic for the two-timing man. I watched as he greedily devoured my fly agaric chocolates one by one, without even looking at them. To think of all the time and effort I had put into them! They could have been generic store-bought chocolates for all he knew or cared. I felt a fresh wave of dislike for the man.

The crowd was gathered around Stan, staring at him. All of a sudden, Stan let out a yell. He jumped to his feet and pointed. "You!"

I spun around, as did the rest of the crowd gathered.

Minnie and Mick were standing close together, talking, or at least they had been.

"How dare you invite that man to my party!" Stan yelled at Minnie. "You gave me your word that you two had broken up!" He made to rise to his feet, but Craig and Miriam managed to restrain him.

"You'd better go," Minnie said to Mick. "I'll call you later."

"You will *not* call him later!" Stan yelled, struggling to his feet once more.

Mick headed for the door, but Stan broke away from Miriam and hurried after him.

"I wonder if there's going to be a fight," Carl whispered in my ear. "I don't like Stan's chances."

"Me either." I looked at Mick's muscular appearance. I knew that sheep shearers were fit and strong, whereas Stan had obviously spent too much time in front of his computer. He didn't strike me as the healthy type. If it did come to a fight, it would be over in seconds.

This must have occurred to Stan because when he reached Mick, he simply shook his fist in front of his face. "I told you to stay away from my daughter, you good for nothing…" He let out a stream of obscene language that made his daughter gasp.

She tugged on her father's arm. "Daddy, stop it. You're making a scene." She nodded to the door. Mick took the hint and hurried out. "I didn't invite him, Daddy," Minnie said, although her tone was less than convincing.

"Then why was he here?" Stan roared.

"I don't know." Minnie shrugged. "I didn't invite him," she added lamely.

Miriam rushed over and took Stan by the arm. "Come

on, Stan, don't let this ruin your lovely evening." She shot a venomous glare at Minnie. "Come on now."

She led him back to the chocolate table. "I was going to present these chocolates to you when we made the speeches, but you've already eaten some of them." She gestured to a chair. "Why don't you eat some more, and I'll get you a drink. Your usual?"

Stan nodded, and sat down, accepting my lovely fly agaric chocolates from Miriam. He continued to shove them in his mouth, not even tasting them. It looked as if he swallowed them whole. I was furious.

Carl, as best friends do, realised why I was upset. "Narel, you can only create the chocolates. You have to release them into the wild, and then you're no longer responsible for how people treat them."

I sighed long and hard. "I know you're right." I looked around the room. Everyone was now ignoring Stan, and several were crowded around Minnie, consoling her. Peaches was still off to one side, clearly forgotten by Stan. I pointed this out to Carl.

"I feel quite sorry for her, not knowing Stan was having an affair with his housekeeper," Carl said. "But then again, if she is truly a gold digger, then she got what she deserved."

"If she is a gold digger, then good luck to her!" I said. "It sounds like Stan deserves her." Before I had even finished my words, Peaches snatched up her purse and stormed across the room to the door. It was a dramatic exit, or would have been, if anyone had paid any attention. Carl and I seem to be the only audience. Stan certainly didn't notice, as he was busy stuffing his face with the chocolates.

"I didn't think anyone could eat so many chocolates in one go," Carl said, "except you, of course, Narel. I think he can eat more chocolates than you can."

I was thinking up a witty retort, when Stan stood up, clutched his stomach, and fell face forward onto the ground. Miriam screamed.

The conversation in the room immediately stopped, replaced at once with an eerie silence.

Miriam, bending over the body, called out for help. Craig and a man I hadn't met were the first ones there. They rolled the body over.

"Is he dead?" Miriam said through her sobs.

The other man checked his pulse. "No. Quick, somebody call an ambulance!"

The nearest woman whipped out her phone and spoke into it. Everything was a blur, with people huddled over Stan. "I think he's had a heart attack," Craig said.

Miriam shook her head. "He's had a terrible stomach flu the last few days, and I didn't even know if he would make it to his party tonight. I told him to drink plenty of fluids. Are you sure he's alive?"

Craig tried to assure her that he was, but Minnie was at once beside Stan, bending over him and sobbing. "It's all my fault," she wailed. "I should have told Mick to leave the second I saw him here. He's upset Daddy, and now Daddy's had a heart attack."

The woman who had called the ambulance patted Minnie on the shoulder somewhat awkwardly. I expected Miriam to console her, but Miriam ignored her completely.

"That was a bit of a shock," Carl said. "Shouldn't someone put a blanket over him or something?"

"It's quite warm in here, though," I said.

Carl shrugged. "That's what they do in movies. Anyway, I expect the ambulance will be here any second."

Carl was right. There was only a short space of time until the paramedics arrived. Miriam asked everyone to leave the room, to give Stan privacy. I had to walk right past Stan, given he was between us and the exit, and I saw that one of my fly agaric chocolates had fallen from his hand.

There was something wrong with it. My chocolates were beautiful replicas of the fly agaric mushroom, all pretty and smooth-topped, red with white spots. This chocolate had a little round white cap on the top. It looked something like a moulded marshmallow, but I certainly hadn't put it there.

We all gathered, huddled in the next room, waiting for news of Stan. I tapped Carl's arm. "You remember what my fly agaric chocolates look like, don't you?"

Carl nodded.

"Stan had one in his hand that he hadn't eaten. It was right next to his hand on the ground. There was something stuck to the top of it."

Carl frowned. "What do you mean?"

"I mean, I think he was poisoned. I think someone put something poisonous on the top of the fly agaric to make it look like part of the chocolate."

Carl disagreed. "Narel, there have been a few murders lately, and that's why you're thinking that. Perhaps it was something on the floor and it just looked like something on top of your chocolate."

I shook my head. "No, it was definitely on top of the

chocolate. I have to get back in there and look at the other chocolates."

"All right, as soon as they take him out, I'll slip back in and have a look. What am I looking for, exactly?"

"Take a photo of them with your phone," I said. "Just the fly agaric chocolates. He wasn't eating anything else, was he?"

Carl shrugged. "I don't think so."

Carl was interrupted by the appearance of the paramedics wheeling out Stan. He was clearly still alive, as he was on a drip. "I'll distract Miriam, while you slip inside and take photos of the fly agaric chocolates and anything else that looks suspicious," I hissed to Carl.

He nodded, and slipped away. "Miriam, how is he?" I said, hurrying to catch up to her.

"They haven't said what's wrong with him," she said, wiping a tear from her eye. "I'm going in the ambulance with him."

I looked around for Carl, but couldn't see him. I decided to go back into the room to fetch him, but I had only taken a few steps when he emerged. "Did you get the photos?" I asked urgently.

Carl shook his head. "There weren't any of those chocolates left."

"No chocolates?" I said in horror.

"No fly agaric chocolates at all," Carl said. "And before you ask, yes, I looked in the box and I looked everywhere, but there were none."

I rubbed my forehead. "That's not possible. I didn't just make enough for one person. It's not possible that he ate every last one of them."

"Are you saying someone took them?" Carl said. "But why would they?"

I rolled my eyes. "Obviously, because the chocolates were poisoned."

"Poisoned with those blobs on the top you were talking about?" Carl said. "Narel, don't you think that's a bit of a stretch? If someone wanted to poison someone, they would simply inject poison into the chocolates."

I thought about that for a moment. "No, Carl. If they had poisoned buttons already, all they had to do was place them on top of the mushrooms. That wouldn't look at all suspicious—it would just look like someone arranging chocolates. Someone could hardly go up with a syringe in front of everyone and inject chocolates."

Carl took my elbow and moved me away from some people who had moved over to us and were talking in hushed tones. When we were standing against the far wall, he continued. "That makes sense, but Narel, we don't even know that Stan was poisoned. It was probably a heart attack. You saw how upset he was."

"I just don't know, Carl. All I know is that I certainly didn't put that button cap on my chocolates, and that means that someone else did."

"Maybe Miriam did, thinking it needed some more decorating," Carl said. "Okay, I realise that sounds lame, but you have to admit it's possible. There's probably a perfectly innocent explanation for it, Narel. You can't see murder around every corner."

Just then, Detectives Clyde and Rieker burst into the room. "Everyone stay where you are," Clyde said.

CHAPTER 4

Carl was the first to react. "You were right, Narel!"

I was too shocked to respond.

The detectives marched straight over to me. "Fancy seeing you at the scene of a crime, Miss Myers," Detective Clyde said rather too smugly.

I glared at him. I had never taken to Detective Clyde. He was just how I imagined Hercule Poirot would look: the same stature and body shape, the same arrogance, right down to the highly polished shoes. All he needed was the waxed moustache.

"A crime?" Carl said. "So he was poisoned then?"

"Alleged crime," Rieker added, smiling at Carl and then glaring at his partner.

Detective Clyde folded his arms over his chest. "Rieker, organise the others while I speak to these two." When Rieker left, Clyde addressed Carl. "What made you think he was poisoned?" His tone was filled with suspicion.

"You're here, the man has been taken away in an

ambulance, and there were no knives sticking out of him, and he wasn't shot. That only leaves poisoning." Carl glared at the man in response.

I couldn't wait to tell the detective what I suspected. "I already suspected that he was poisoned, and I only just finished telling Carl about it." I looked at Carl, and he nodded. I pushed on. "Miriam Moreton, Stan Wellings' secretary, ordered a lot of handmade chocolates for this event, and she wanted to present him with some very special ones. I handmade some fly agaric chocolates—you know, the red and white toadstools that elves and fairies sit on?" He just looked blank, so I continued. "The thing is, Miriam was supposed to present them to Mr Wellings later, but he ate a whole bunch of them. When he fell on the ground, one fell out of his hand, and it had something stuck to the top. I certainly hadn't put anything on top of the chocolates I made, so someone else did it."

I thought he would dismiss what I said, but he did not. "What exactly did this look like?"

"It looked a bit like a marshmallow, only more of a solid white and round like a cap." I held my hands to demonstrate the shape and the size. "It definitely was sitting on top of the chocolate and I definitely didn't put it there. I didn't make any chocolates that shape at all."

"Wait here." With that, Clyde disappeared into the room.

Carl looked white and shaken. "Narel, you were right. Someone tried to kill him, after all. I wonder how the paramedics were onto it so quickly?"

"Symptoms, I suppose."

"But he wasn't foaming at the mouth or anything, was

he?" Carl said. "He just fell flat on his face and he was unconscious."

"Oh well, paramedics know more than we do. They must have seen something to make them call the cops."

Clyde hurried back to me. "Were you the last to leave the room?"

I shook my head. "I was probably about halfway in the group. I almost forgot. I sent Carl back in to take photos on his phone of the other fly agaric chocolates, but they were all gone. And Carl didn't see that one on the ground, did you, Carl?"

Carl shook his head. "No, I looked all over the floor to see if it rolled somewhere, but that chocolate was gone and the thing on the top was gone, and there wasn't a single fly agaric chocolate left in the box."

Detective Clyde tapped his pen on his notepad. "Maybe someone ate them all."

"No, that's just it," I said. "They were in a box, and they were special ones just for Stan Wellings. I could see him from where I was and he was the only one eating them. There were too many for him to eat all in one go. That means someone must have taken the others as well as the one on the ground."

"Are you sure there were some left in the box?" he asked me.

I thought back. "I couldn't see the contents of the box from where I was, but I saw him shoving them into his mouth. There was no way he could have eaten them all, because Miriam asked me to make a large quantity, I suppose so Stan had enough for a week or so. Sure he was shovelling them down his throat at a great rate of knots, but he couldn't have eaten them all. No one could." *No one but me,* I added silently.

"Wait here," Clyde said again. This time, he hurried over to speak to Rieker, who had directed everyone to sit on seats at the other side of the room. Miriam was still clearly distressed, and was being comforted by Craig. Minnie was being comforted by two women I hadn't met.

After a short interval, Clyde came back to me. "Could you draw this item for me?"

"Sure."

Clyde took me into a side room and I did my best to draw the object, complete with the fly agaric chocolate. The detective seemed somewhat disappointed with my artwork. "Basically, it was a blob?" he asked me.

I shook my head, affronted. "No, it wasn't a blob, not like frosting. It held its shape. It was like a round thing, like a dome."

"And how far away from this object were you, Miss Myers?"

"From me to that wall over there," I said, gesturing to the far wall. "But I saw it clearly. After all, it was on one of my chocolates and I hadn't put it there."

"And did you see similar objects on top of all the other special chocolates?"

I had to think about that. "Actually, I only saw him dip his hand in the box and then shovel them into his mouth," I said. "I wouldn't have seen anything at all, whether those blobs were there or not."

Clyde appeared to be thinking it over. "All right then, Miss Myers. You can join the others and we will take your witness statement presently, after the forensics team arrives."

I walked back into the main room and stood next to Carl, who in turn was standing next to a huge potted fern.

"Look, it's that nosy local reporter," Carl said. "Graham Gibson. How did he get wind of it so quickly?"

I shrugged. "Perhaps he listens into police radio like they do on TV."

Carl was about to respond, but didn't have the chance, because Graham Gibson hightailed it over to us. "Narel Myers, I presume?" he said in a smug manner.

"Yes," I said.

He looked Carl up and down. "Nice to see you again, Carl," he said in a tone that made it very clear that he wasn't at all pleased to see Carl.

Carl simply glared at him and did not respond.

"I haven't been back in town long, but I've been doing my research," he said. "Narel, if I may call you Narel?" Without waiting for me to answer, he continued. "Narel, you have been implicated in every recent murder in this town haven't you?"

"She hasn't been implicated," Carl snapped. "It's just that she happened to be around one or two of them. She was never a suspect."

The man simply smirked. "And this time, a man has been taken away, poisoned, after eating chocolates you made, Narel."

"I didn't poison the chocolates," I sputtered, but Graham simply smirked at me.

"Let's look at the facts," he said in a snarky manner. "A man is poisoned, possibly with a fatal outcome. He ate your chocolates before he keeled over. Therefore, the chocolates were poisoned. Whether you poisoned them or not is another matter, and whether you poisoned them deliberately or not is another matter still."

I was struck speechless. Apparently so was Carl, because the two of us stood there wordlessly. Thankfully, Detective Rieker came over. "I'll take your statement now, Carl," he said with a big smile. I thought he winked at Carl, but I couldn't be certain. I excused myself from the reporter and went to sit on a vacant seat in the middle of the group. I happened to look up to see the reporter was taking photos of me with his iPhone and I instinctively put up my hand to cover my face.

Graham Gibson smiled, and then walked away. Several people, I assume the forensics team, arrived and Clyde spoke to them in hushed tones before opening the door to the reception room.

This was turning out to be quite a nightmare. The police seemed to think it was poison, and that nosy reporter had also thought it was poison, but then again he might have been clutching at straws in his attempt to write a sensationalist story. Still, it was clear that the police were treating it as attempted murder, so that did suggest that Stan had ingested poison. If it hadn't been in the wine, then it had to be in my chocolates. I knew I didn't poison the chocolates, so someone else did. But who?

I looked around the room. It was likely I was sitting in the presence of an attempted murderer, unless of course that person had been Mick Holder, as he left after the altercation with Stan. Oh, and then there was the housekeeper, Daphne Delamare, who had left after her altercation with Stan.

I sighed and put my head in my hands. This had certainly been an eventful night, and it wasn't over yet.

Carl presently returned, but before I had a chance to speak to him, Detective Clyde whisked me away to give my witness statement. I wondered why they didn't ask us to give our statements down at the station, but I suppose there were so many of us, and they wanted the events fresh in our minds, given that, no doubt, one of us was the murderer.

I sat opposite Detective Clyde in a small office, and wiped my sweaty palms on my dress. I felt nervous, like I was here for a job interview. The office was clinical, all white and steel, and the furniture looked as though it had been purchased from a cheap flat pack furniture store. Then were numerous potted palms, but I couldn't tell from where I was sitting if they were artificial or not. I guess that they were, given they looked far too green and shiny. Real plants indoors never looked quite that good. The view out the window was of the neighbouring rooftops, as far as I could tell in the cloud-covered moonlight. An owl, or some other large night bird, flew past, causing me to jump.

After I had gone through the events yet again with Clyde, he asked, "And what was your relationship with Stan Wellings?"

I shook my head. "I had never met him. The only person I met before I came here was Miriam Moreton, his personal secretary. She was the one who ordered all the chocolates for this retirement party."

"I saw they were all specific shapes. Did Miriam Moreton decide the shapes?"

"Yes. She wanted several red Porsches to match his car,

and she wanted the fly agarics. She also wanted sports bikes, but she said I could make up other shapes. Those were the specific ones she requested."

He nodded. "So red Porsches because he owned one?"

"That's right," I said.

He tapped his pen. "And why sports bikes?"

I shrugged. "I can't remember. I think she said he had those, too."

"And why fly agaric?"

"That was connected with some big deal he made, the one that made him rich," I said. "You'd have to ask Miriam. It was some big contract he got doing a huge advertising promotion for a video game."

"I see. And if you didn't know anyone, Miss Myers, why were you still there?"

I didn't know what he meant, and I said so.

"I mean, why didn't you simply deliver the chocolates and go home? Why did you stay at the party?"

"Because I had to look after the chocolate fountain," I said. "You have to keep adding chocolate to it as people consume at. Someone has to be with the chocolate fountain. It's not something you can just switch on and leave." I jumped to my feet and clapped my hand over my mouth.

Clyde looked alarmed. "What is it?"

"I have to turn the machine off!" I said in horror. "If all the chocolate has hardened it will burn out the motor. I have to put it onto the low setting at once or my machine will be ruined! That's an expensive piece of equipment!"

"Sit down, Miss Myers."

I did as I was asked. "Please, you have to let me in there or the chocolate fountain will be ruined."

Clyde appeared to be thinking over my request. "All

right then, I'll go with you, but you must be careful not to touch anything"

When I emerged from the office, Carl raised his eyebrows, but I simply said, "Chocolate fountain," as I walked past him. The forensics team had already bagged most of my chocolates, but the chocolate fountain was still running. I hurried over to the settings. To my horror, the chocolate had hardened. I turned to Detective Clyde. "Are they going to take my fountain? Or just some of the chocolate? It's just that this fountain cost me quite a bit of money and I have to work fast to fix this."

"I'll check." The detective walked away and spoke to a woman in a white suit before returning. "They've already taken a sample of that chocolate, so do what you have to do. Just make sure you don't touch anything else at all. I'll be here, watching you."

I set the fountain control knob to *Heat Only*, and waited until the chocolate started to melt.

"Have you finished yet, Miss Myers?" Detective Clyde said, clearly impatient. "This *is* a murder investigation, you know."

"Murder?" I echoed, and spun around. "Is Mr Wellings dead?"

Clyde flushed bright red. "Sorry, force of habit. I meant to say it's an *attempted* murder investigation."

His tone was not at all convincing, and I was left wondering if there was something he wasn't telling me.

CHAPTER 5

I couldn't wait to tell Carl. By the time I got to the other room, everyone but Carl had left. He didn't seem interested in my news. "He probably *did* mean to say attempted murder, you know," he said, after I had relayed the detective's words to him.

I shook my head. "I'm not so sure."

"Anyway, this could be the least of our worries."

I was puzzled. "What you mean, Carl?"

"It's that ghastly reporter, Graham Gibson."

I had almost forgotten about the reporter. "Oh yes, you two had met, hadn't you?"

Carl's face turned a pale shade of green. "It was when you were recovering in the hospital in Sydney. He was here for a month or two, and he seemed to take a dislike to me. He did a big front page article on me at the Mardi Gras."

"And that upset you?"

Carl's face turned an even more sickly shade of green. "Narel, you have simply *no* idea what I was wearing at the

Mardi Gras. The photo was taken from a *most* unflattering angle, and the article was along the lines of, *Do you trust this man with your files?*"

"Oh Carl, that's so awful! Why didn't you tell me?"

Carl made a snorting sound. "I'd hardly tell you, Narel, what with you being close to death and having all those surgeries. I'm so sorry he's back in town, though, because he's a real troublemaker."

The following morning, I found out just how much of a troublemaker Graham Gibson was. I had awoken earlier than normal, probably due to the previous night's events. Still, Mongrel expected to be fed as soon as I woke up, no matter what time that was. I staggered out into the kitchen and switched on the coffee machine before reaching for Mongrel's dry food.

I went through my early morning routine like a robot, feeding Mongrel, and then having a light breakfast of coffee and chocolate. I knew I had to get healthy, so lately I had been adding a banana to my morning routine.

I had also decided I needed to buy another house. My current house was tiny and cramped, and I could now afford a nicer house. I had considered renovating this one, but by the time I paid for all the renovations, I would have spent more than the house was worth. It simply made sense to buy a nice new house that would not need anything doing to it. I was always having trouble with the drains here. In fact, I often said for a joke that I kept the local plumber in business.

In my spare time, I had taken to looking at houses for sale online. Of course, it would have been far easier to call on Borage, the local real estate agent, but he hadn't called since we had been on a dinner date. That was only recently, but it made it all a little awkward.

I had considered going back to bed, but I knew I wouldn't sleep, and if I did, I was afraid of sleeping through the alarm and not opening the shop on time. I decided to have another coffee and then a shower. I wondered what had become of the Cat Whisperer, and if I would ever hear from him again.

I had just put on my work clothes when there was a loud banging on my front door. I hoped it wasn't the police. I hurried to the door and flung it open, and then let out a long sigh of relief when I saw Carl standing there. I wasn't so relieved when I took another look. Carl's face was white and drawn. "What's happened?" I asked him urgently.

Carl staggered inside and threw himself on my sofa. "Look!" he said dramatically, thrusting a newspaper into my hands.

I gasped. There, across the front of the local newspaper was the headline, *Local Shop Owner Suspected in Heinous Crime*. The photo, which took up half the page, was of me shielding my face. "I remember when he took that photo," I said angrily. "Carl, it makes me look guilty."

"No it doesn't," Carl said lamely.

I threw myself on the sofa next to Carl. "Can I sue him?"

Carl's jaw dropped open. "Sue? Sue a newspaper? I'm sure they don't have to tell the truth."

I shook my head. "Seriously, they can't make wild accusations like that. Do you think I should see a lawyer?"

Carl looked off into the distance. "Maybe, I don't

know. Wouldn't you have to prove that you weren't a suspect?"

My hands flew to my throat. "Carl, you don't think I'm a suspect, do you?"

Carl stood up. "I need coffee, Narel. This is too early in the morning for me."

I raised my eyebrows. "But it's just after eight."

"Exactly," Carl said over his shoulder as he staggered in the direction of the coffee machine.

"I think I remembered somewhere that if you can prove a false allegation has negatively affected your business, then you can sue," I called after him. "At least I have the money to sue."

Carl downed a short black before speaking. "That would be a waste of money. Just ignore him. I'm sure he wants attention, and nobody in town will believe his outrageous lies. My advice is to go to your chocolate shop as normal and carry on as if nothing has happened."

"What if people *do* think my chocolates poisoned him?" I said. "This chocolate shop is my dream." I read some more of the article, and my throat constricted. "Where did he get all this information?" I jabbed my finger viciously on the newspaper. "He says that Stan Wellings fell to the ground after eating my chocolates. The article says that he's in a critical condition and the police have ruled it as attempted murder. Carl, what if all my customers leave?"

Carl poured himself another short black. "Oh Narel, I'm sure it won't come to that. If it makes you feel any better, I'll come with you to work today. By the way, that Miriam woman did pay you in advance for all those chocolates, didn't she?"

"Yes, she did. I feel sorry for her."

Carl returned to the living room and took me by my shoulders. "Now, you listen to me, Narel. That woman could be a cold-blooded murderer for all you know. Save your sympathy for yourself and for me."

"So you think we *are* suspects then?"

Carl shrugged. "Maybe in theory. Everyone that was at the party would have to be a suspect, in theory. I'm sure those detectives don't think we had anything to do with it, and they'll solve the attempted murder sooner or later."

That prompted my memory of what Detective Clyde had said the previous night. "Carl, I know you didn't think he meant anything by it, but Detective Clyde went all funny just after he said it was a murder investigation."

Carl was already back in the kitchen, now looking through my cupboards. "Do you have anything in here to eat besides chocolate, Narel? Okay, I see you have some fruit. That's a good start. Just because you can't put on any weight doesn't mean you shouldn't be healthy, you know."

"I know, I know. I'm working on it, seriously. Now, did you hear what I just said?"

Carl gave up his search and sat down with a banana and an apple. "Are you thinking that Detective Clyde knew Stan had already died, but didn't want to tell anyone, maybe to trick the murderer somehow?"

I shrugged. "That makes sense. I really don't have any idea. Never mind, Carl—it was probably just my imagination. Anyway, let's get going to the shop."

By ten that morning, not a single customer had entered my shop, not a local customer, anyway. I had several people on their way to the Sunshine Coast, and another set of tourists. Nevertheless, Carl was trying to do his best to maintain an upbeat attitude. "Don't worry about it, Narel! You've made some good money already."

I shook my head. "Carl, this place can't exist on tourists alone. I need the locals as well for bread and butter money."

"Think of it this way," Carl said smiling, although the smile did not reach his eyes, "it will give you more time to work on your online chocolate store. How is that going, by the way?"

I exhaled loudly and sat on a seat behind the counter. "I'm getting there. It's just that life keeps getting in the way of my plans. I have to buy a new house too, and I can't leave it much longer because the old one's falling down about my ears."

"The house is an easy fix. Just call in and see your good buddy, Porridge."

I shook my finger at Carl in warning. "Please never say that word again."

Carl snickered. "You have to admit, it's kind of a strange name. I don't know why he didn't just stick with good old Tom Fletcher."

"In a word, bullying," I said. "Have you already forgotten what *The Populars* put all of us through in school? I don't blame him for changing his name."

"And have you forgotten that all *The Populars* were murdered?" Carl said. "There's no reason to keep calling himself Porridge any longer."

"You're right." The deep voice came from behind us.

I could have simply died on the spot. I wanted the ground to open up and swallow me, and all those other sayings one uses at such a time as this. To say I was mortified was an understatement.

There, standing behind Carl, was Borage Fletcher.

He looked amused, or that might have been just suppressed anger. "You're right," he said again. "I've decided to go back to my old name, Tom."

I just stood there, opening and closing my mouth like a fish, but Carl had the presence of mind to speak. "Good, that's a much better name. I much prefer Tom to Borage."

Then again, maybe it wasn't such a good idea that Carl spoke.

To my great relief, Borage, I mean Tom, laughed. "I didn't like the name either; it's just that I didn't want anyone to know I was that little Tom Fletcher from high school."

"But all those people who bullied you are now dead," Carl said cheerfully. I suppose he was trying to be helpful.

"Err, yes." It seemed as if Tom didn't know how to take that statement. He turned to me. "How are you, Narel? Sorry I haven't called. I just got back to town this morning. Do you remember all that trouble my brother and sister-in-law were having?"

I was still unable to speak, so I simply nodded.

"I had to go out west to sort things out. There's no internet or even phone connection out there. I left in a hurry, and didn't think I'd be away as long as I was, or I would have let you know first."

I kept nodding. I felt like an idiot, but I was still shocked that Tom had overheard Carl complaining about his name.

"You know," Carl said, "I'm so used to calling you Borage that I'm going to find it hard to call you Tom."

I finally found my voice. "I like both names," I lied, "but I have to agree with Carl. I'll probably call you Borage a few times before I get used to calling you Tom again, like I did back in school."

Borage/Tom waved a hand in dismissal. "That doesn't matter at all. Call me anything you like." He winked at me, and my knees went weak. I grabbed the counter top. "How about coffee sometime soon?" he asked me.

"She might as well have coffee with you now, and I'll mind the store," Carl said. "There won't be any customers for the rest of the day if this morning has been anything to go by."

Tom raised his eyebrows. "Why is that?"

Carl's hand flew to his mouth. "Oh, you wouldn't have heard yet, would you? You just got back to town this morning?" Without waiting for Tom to answer, he pushed on. "And you haven't seen the papers?" After Tom shook his head, Carl said, "Narel provided handmade chocolates for a local ad executive's retirement party last night, and he had a heart attack or something after he ate one, only it wasn't a heart attack, it was poisoning. At least, we think it was poisoning because there were no knives or guns involved, and the detectives came. You know, that mean Detective Clyde and that super hot Detective Rieker?"

I held up my hand to stop Carl speaking, as I was sure he was confusing Tom. "Stan Wellings had a retirement party last night at their office. I made the chocolates, and I also made a special box of chocolates just for him. He stuffed his face with those, because he had an argument…"

Carl interrupted me. "He had two arguments, Narel."

I nodded. "Yes, he had two arguments, but my point was that he stuffed his face with the special chocolates I made and then fell to the floor. The paramedics came and then the cops came, too."

"You're involved with another murder?" Tom said incredulously. He must have seen my expression, because he hurried to add, "Not that it's any of your fault, of course, Narel."

I pursed my lips. "Quite so. Anyway, we're pretty sure he was poisoned, because..."

Carl interrupted me again. "Because he wasn't shot, and there was no knife sticking out of his back. Although perhaps someone stuck a syringe of insulin or something into him when no one else was looking."

I groaned and rubbed my forehead. "Carl, he probably would have noticed if someone jabbed him with a syringe. Anyway, can I please speak?" Carl waved a hand at me to continue. "Borage, sorry, I mean Tom, do you know what fly agaric mushrooms look like?"

Tom thought for a moment, and then said, "Aren't they those red ones with the white spots, the ones you see in illustrations with elves sitting on them?"

I nodded. "Yes, that's right. His secretary had especially asked me to make some like that, but I didn't put any tops on them. I mean, obviously I put the red and white mushroom tops on them, but I didn't put anything on top of those. When Stan fell to the floor, there was a fly agaric chocolate next to him and it had a dome stuck on the top. And what's more, I told the detectives that, but they couldn't find the fly agaric chocolate at all, and the ones left in the box were missing."

Tom rubbed his chin. "Yes, that does sound like poisoning. It sounds as if that dome on the top contained the poison which someone had pre-prepared simply to stick on a chocolate. And you say he was helping himself to the box?"

I tried to remember. "I think his daughter might've handed him the box, but he was going to eat them at some point anyway, because they were especially for him. In fact, Miriam was annoyed that he was eating them before they were officially presented to him."

"Who's Miriam?" Tom asked me.

"Oh, sorry. Miriam Moreton is Stan's personal secretary. She organised his retirement party and seemed to have a high opinion of him. I later heard he was quite unpopular."

"He was obviously unpopular with one person, at least," Tom said dryly.

Carl clearly thought Tom's remark enormously funny and slapped him on the back.

CHAPTER 6

I sat with Tom in the nearest café. It wasn't a particularly romantic café, but it was the closest to my shop. Carl promised he would call if too many customers for him to handle arrived, but I really didn't think that would happen.

Butterflies went crazy in my stomach as I sat across from Tom. This was one of my first dates, rather a sad fact if you considered my age. It was even sadder that my very first date had said some unkind words to me, got into his car out the front of the restaurant, and then exploded along with his car. My second dinner date was actually with Tom, and on that occasion the police had dragged me away for questioning. I sure hoped this coffee date would pass uneventfully.

I fidgeted and took in my surroundings. I had been in here many times before. It was not particularly intimate, nor did it have any kind of ambience about it. The decor was mostly black and white, with big black square tiles on the floor, and numerous hanging lights, half of which weren't working. The front wall was entirely made of glass, letting in plenty of natural light.

"Are you all right, Narel?" Tom asked me. "You seem a million miles away."

"Sorry." I wrung my hands. "It's just that the paper did a terrible article about me this morning, and said I was the main suspect in the crime."

Tom frowned. "Don't worry, everyone knows the local paper is now just a sensationalist bunch of nonsense. No one will take it seriously."

I disagreed. "Saturday morning is usually very busy for me, with people out and about at the weekend. Not a single person has come into the shop so far today—tourists, sure, but not a single local."

Tom shrugged. "That's probably a coincidence. I bet Carl will call at any moment, saying he's swamped with customers."

I forced a smile. "Possibly. I wonder how Stan Wellings is doing. Actually, I wonder who poisoned him. I hope the police solve the crime soon, or I'm sure I won't have any customers."

"Weren't you starting an online business?" Tom asked me.

"Carl asked me that too, just before you came in." I was beginning to wonder whether the question indicated that Carl and Tom thought an online business would soon be my only income. Truth be told, I didn't need an income because the settlement had been enough to set me up for life. The insurance company of the drunk driver who had hit my car and nearly killed me had paid me a handsome sum, but I didn't want to sit around and watch TV all day. I wanted my little chocolate shop to succeed.

Our coffee and cake arrived, and I thought it best to change the subject. "Borage, oh sorry, I mean Tom, I want to buy another house." As soon as I said it, I silently berated myself. I didn't want to talk shop—this was supposed to be a date of sorts.

"Are you going to sell your current house or keep it as an investment house?"

I made a small choking sound, and then realised that was likely a most unattractive thing to do. "No, I'm going to sell it. If I kept it, it would continue to be a money pit. The plumbing's on its way out, and so is most of the rest of the place, truth be told. I'll sell it for a bargain price; I just want to get rid of it."

"Do you have any idea what part of town you'd like to live in? And what are you looking for in a house?"

I shrugged. "I want a fairly new house, preferably one still under builder's warranty. My current house has been such a nightmare with all the constant repairs, all the roof leaks, the drains being blocked, the termite damage. I could go on. I just want something nice and new, and preferably within walking distance of Carl's place, because he's my best friend. I'd like it nice and leafy, with established trees."

Tom sipped his coffee before speaking. "How many bedrooms?"

"Well, there's only me, and Mongrel."

Tom laughed. "I'm sure Mongrel doesn't need his own bedroom."

I laughed, too. "No, so two bedrooms would be fine. Or maybe three, I don't know. I am serious about starting the online chocolate business, though, so it would be good to have a room I could use as a home office."

"And how has Mongrel been going? Has he put anyone else in hospital lately?" Tom obviously meant it as a joke, but I had news for him.

"Yesterday, actually."

Tom nearly choked on his cake. He managed to swallow it, and asked, "Seriously? What happened?"

"Well, it was quite bizarre," I said. "Last week, Carl was over for dinner, and we had just finished the first course of chocolate glazed pumpkin risotto, when someone knocked on the door. It was a guy going door to door, some famous Cat Whisperer. He asked if I had any cats with behavioural problems."

Tom thought that was particularly funny. "He sure was in luck at your place."

I shook my head. "That was just it. I didn't think anyone could possibly help Mongrel, so I was about to send him away, but Carl got very excited and said he'd buy his services for me as a gift. Then the poor guy came yesterday afternoon. It all started out well enough, but he wanted to do extinction therapy with Mongrel."

Tom went white. "You don't mean…?" His voice trailed away.

I nodded solemnly. "Yes. It was only a small piece of rope, but it was enough. I don't think he needed too many stitches. I think he just went into shock."

Tom leant across the table. "Hey, what was his name?"

"Peter Patterson. Apparently he's quite famous, if you can believe what he says. Still, my father always said that self praise is no recommendation. This Cat Whisperer guy even has a documentary series on cat training. He calls himself The Purr-suader."

Tom slapped his hand on the table. "I've heard of him!

I saw an interview with him on TV recently. He's had an interesting life. He loved cats for as long as he can remember, and in fact, he met his wife at a cat show. He bred Abyssinians, and she bred Himalayans. She ran off with another man, someone he worked with, and then had a child or children with him, and then died ten or so years later. He never married again, poor guy. I had the feeling that he never got over her."

"That's sad," I said. "Still, why would such a famous Cat Whisperer who has his own TV show and everything come to our small country town and go door to door with fancy brochures?"

Tom drained the last of his coffee. After he set down his cup on the table, he said, "It does seem quite strange, doesn't it? Perhaps he was visiting relatives in town. Anyway, I'll bet those brochures were real fancy."

I was puzzled. "Yes they were, but how did you know?"

"He was an advertising executive in Sydney for many years before he became a Cat Whisperer, according to the documentary," Tom said.

My synapses sparked, making connection after connection. "Tom! I wonder—oh no, it's probably too much of a coincidence. But Tom!" Before Tom could speak, I added, "Stan Wellings is an advertising executive, and he came from Sydney. His wife died some years ago. Sure, I know Sydney has like, five million people, but what if Stan's wife was the love of Peter Patterson's life? What if The Purr-suader poisoned Stan Wellings?"

Tom looked doubtful. "It does seem a bit of a coincidence."

I was on a roll. "But don't you see? He had access to the chocolates, the fly agaric chocolates. He was in the kitchen by himself. He could have easily poisoned those chocolates."

"But didn't you say there was a dome-like object on the top? You would have noticed if that had suddenly appeared."

"True." I tapped my chin. "Perhaps he injected the chocolates with poison in my kitchen, and that dome-like cap on the top was something entirely innocent."

"Did he know the fly agaric chocolates were specifically for Stan Wellings?"

I thought about it. "Yes, actually, he did. Well no, I didn't mention Stan's name at all, but I did specifically tell him that the fly agaric chocolates were a special gift for an office retirement party that night. I said the other chocolates were for everyone, but these were specifically for the person who was retiring."

"Narel, you should tell the police."

I readily agreed. "I'll call them after we have coffee." I regretted bringing up the subject. The romance in my life had to date been pretty thin, non-existent to tell the truth, and this was my first taste of it now. I hoped I hadn't ruined what could have been a pleasant time with Tom by first bringing up my search for a new house, and then an attempted murder.

Tom looked at his watch. "Narel, I've got to run. I have an open home soon, and I'm running late to get it ready."

I hoped my disappointment wasn't showing on my face. I also hoped Tom didn't think I had friend-zoned him, and I even more fervently hoped he hadn't friend-zoned me.

"I'm quite busy as I've been out of town for a while, but I'd love to have dinner again soon?"

His question took me by surprise. "Um, err, um, that would be lovely," I stammered.

"How was your romantic time with Porridge?" Carl asked as soon as I set foot in my shop, a shop which sadly was empty.

"Call him Tom now, Carl," I said sternly. "It was dreadful; I did all the wrong things. I talked about wanting to buy a house, and then I talked about the attempted murder."

Carl busied himself polishing a glass cabinet. "Hardly the most romantic things to talk about."

I frowned at him. "You're supposed to say it didn't matter, that he likes me anyway."

Carl sighed dramatically. "Of course he likes you, Narel. He's probably attracted to your weirdness."

I bit my lip, trying to decide whether or not that was a compliment. "Oh, guess what!" I told Carl what Tom had told me about the Cat Whisperer.

Carl was silent for a long time, which was unusual for him. Finally, he spoke. "It seems a bit of a stretch, doesn't it? And surely if he had injected something into those chocolates, it would have been something that killed him, not just made him sick."

"But remember that Detective Clyde said it was a murder investigation?"

"I still maintain that was probably a slip of the tongue."

I was getting anxious. "Carl, were there any customers while I was having coffee with Tom?"

Carl shook his head. "Sorry, Narel."

I stabbed my finger at my photo splashed across the front of the newspaper. "Carl, we have to solve this murder. I'm sure the police will solve it eventually, but my chocolate shop will be closed by then. Time is of the essence."

Carl stopped polishing and looked up at me. "What do you propose that we do? Are you going to get me into another sticky situation, Narel?"

I ignored that remark. "I think we should go to the hospital, and find out exactly what Stan Wellings was poisoned with. We also need to find out whether he is, in fact, still alive, and if he is, we need to know the extent of his condition."

Carl looked worried. "How are we going to do that?"

I shrugged. "We'll play it by ear."

"When?"

I smiled. "There's no time like the present."

"But what about the shop?" Carl squeaked.

"It's Saturday. We were going to shut at twelve, anyway."

CHAPTER 7

I dragged a still protesting Carl towards the large sliding doors of the hospital entrance. It wasn't as if I was fond of hospitals, quite the contrary. I had spent many months in one in Sydney, and had endured many surgeries, but the fact that a hospital had saved my life didn't make me any happier to enter one.

I'm sure the smell of hospital disinfectant was imperceptible to most people, but I clutched my stomach as a wave of revulsion swamped me. The noises, the nurses' uniforms, the bright lights, all brought memory after memory tumbling back to assault me.

Carl clutched my arm. "Are you all right, Narel?"

"Yes, well, no actually."

"It's not too late to change your mind," he offered hopefully.

I shook my head. I was firm in my resolve. Although the amount I had been awarded in the settlement was large, I had to live on it for the rest of my life, and apart from that, I really wanted my little chocolate shop to succeed for emotional as well as financial reasons. The bullies at school had said I would never amount to anything, and maybe I was trying to prove them wrong. Who knows? I wasn't a psychiatrist. All I knew was that I couldn't bear my chocolate shop to go broke just because of a mean-spirited sensationalist reporter and suspicious local townspeople. If the police weren't going to solve the murder in double quick time, then I would have to do it.

"I assume he's in intensive care," I said to Carl, who simply nodded and looked dismayed.

As we rounded the corner into a wide corridor, Carl caught my arm. "Isn't that Stan's daughter, Minnie?"

Carl had stopped, so I did, too. "Yes, I think it is," I said. "Oh no, do you think her father died? She's sobbing, and there are two nurses comforting her."

"It doesn't look good," Carl said grimly. "Either he's passed away, or he's taken a turn for the worse. We can't walk past her, or she might see us and ask what we're doing here."

I looked around me. "Is there another way to get to the intensive care ward?"

Carl looked around the signs as well. "If there is, I don't know it, and we can hardly ask anyone, not a doctor or nurse anyway. We can't let anyone catch onto what we're doing here. Okay, Narel, let's walk past her as fast as we can and keep to the wall. She's probably too upset to notice her surroundings, anyway."

We managed to get past Minnie without being detected, and followed the signs to the intensive care unit. "Look as if you know where you're going and don't make eye contact with anyone," I hissed at Carl.

To my surprise, it worked. We made it through the

corridors, which were surprisingly labyrinthine for such a small hospital. "Carl, what if he's been transferred to Sydney?"

"I didn't think of that," Carl said hopefully. "That will stop us getting arrested, at any rate. I don't want Detective Rieker to think I'm some sort of common criminal."

"Aha! So that explains your reluctance."

Carl didn't have a chance to respond, because he caught my arm and pulled me back from a corner. "There are cops around that corner, uniformed officers, and a doctor. The police must be guarding Stan Wellings' room," he whispered. "Shush, maybe we can overhear what they say."

We both leant as close to the corner as we dared, and strained our ears. That soon proved to be unnecessary, because the officers' loud tones echoed along the empty corridor.

"He just accused Daphne Delamare, his housekeeper," one voice said. "He came out of his coma, blamed Daphne Delamare, and then died."

Another voice spoke up. "That is normal in the case of death cap mushroom poisoning."

Carl hissed in my ear. "He didn't say fly agaric mushrooms, did he?"

I shook my head. "He said death cap, or something like that." I held my finger to my lips.

"The detectives will be here any minute," a voice said.

Carl and I looked at each other in horror. "Where can we hide?" I asked Carl.

Carl looked aghast. "Are you out of your mind? We're not going to hide—we're going to hightail it out of here before the detectives catch us."

I grabbed Carl by the arm and pulled him inside the nearest room. At least, I thought it was a room until we were in there, because the door had a sign saying *Equipment* on it. It turned out to be a cupboard full of mops and brooms, and I mean full. There was very little room to move, and Carl and I indulged in a childlike game of elbowing each other before we settled down.

"We won't be able to hear anything in here," Carl whispered in my ear.

"Exactly, that's why we have to go out as soon as we hear the detectives walk past."

"How will we know it's the detectives walking past?" Carl hissed. "It could be nurses, or anyone."

"That's a risk we'll have to take," I said in a tone that belied my fear. The pit of my stomach was hollow and I had broken into a cold sweat. I could feel myself trembling. My breath was coming rapidly. I clutched my stomach as a wave of nausea hit me. *Get a grip,* I silently counselled myself.

Just when I thought I couldn't bear it any longer, two sets of loud footsteps stomped past. I shot a look at Carl, and he nodded. We waited a moment, and then climbed out of the tiny room, managing to right several brooms and mops as we did.

We crept back to the corner. Carl went to peek around, but I pulled him back and shook my head. He shrugged and pointed to the corner, but I shook my head more strongly.

Detective Clyde was speaking in his usual strident tone, and for once I was grateful for that. Also, the acoustics in hospital corridors were hardly those of a recording studio.

"No, Detective Clyde, I *can* only give you an approximate timing. He wasn't in good health, but it also depended on how many death caps he had eaten. You'll have to wait until you get the coroner's report."

"Well, please do your best to give me an *approximate* timing." I almost smiled, because I could imagine the frustrated look on Clyde's face.

"He arrived in the hospital at the terminal phase. He had kidney failure, but his death was caused by liver failure."

"Yes, but do you have any idea when he was administered the poison?" Clyde continued in the same frustrated voice.

"As I said, he arrived at the hospital in the terminal phase. There is a so-called recovery phase before that which lasts for two or three days. The patient appears to recover because their symptoms ease. Prior to that, the patient will have stomach pains and vomiting." The doctor's voice was quite matter-of-fact.

"Is it possible the victim was administered the poison just hours before he was brought in?" It was Detective Rieker's voice this time. There was silence for a moment, before the doctor spoke again. "Symptoms could start as early as six hours after a meal of death cap mushrooms..."

Detective Clyde interrupted him. "So then, he could have been poisoned hours before he was brought here?"

Again, the doctor was silent for a few moments before speaking. "No. As I just explained, when the patient first consumes death cap mushrooms, and let us assume it is a significant meal, the patient will suffer symptoms which could be mistaken for stomach flu. These symptoms will usually continue for a day or two. At that point, the symptoms go away and this recovery phase could last for two or three days. After that, the terminal phase kicks in."

"Is this unusual?" Clyde asked him.

"If you mean poisoning by death cap mushrooms, then yes, it *is* quite unusual in these parts," the doctor said, "but I did my residency in Canberra, so I'm familiar with it."

"Then why weren't you able to save him? No offence intended," Detective Rieker added.

"As I explained to you not long after he was admitted, at that point, patients can't be saved. There is a new experimental drug, but it can't be administered after the kidneys have already failed, and in this case, it was too late to save this patient."

"One of the witnesses reported seeing him consume something that looked like a death cap mushroom," Clyde said. "But that was only an hour or so before he was admitted to hospital."

"He had to have eaten the death cap mushroom in significant quantities several days earlier," the doctor said. "It's also clear that he ate more the night he was admitted, but that only served to push him over the edge and hasten his death. Yet whether or not he ate them last evening, the outcome for him would have been the same. It was just a matter of when."

"We'll need to take a statement from you, Dr Marshall. But for now, can you tell us the exact words he used before he died?" The voice was Rieker's.

"He said, 'My housekeeper did it.'"

"Did he name the housekeeper?" Rieker asked him.

"Yes, sorry. His exact words were, 'Daphne did it. My housekeeper, Daphne, did it."

"Thank you, Doctor Marshall, that will be all for now,"

Clyde said. "We'll need to speak with you again at some point."

Carl grabbed my arm and we spun around, but we heard footsteps coming from the other way. I opened the cupboard door and pulled Carl into it. I stood there, trying to calm my breathing so that the detectives wouldn't hear me. I was sure they would hear my heart—it was beating out of my chest. Carl and I clung to each other in fear. I knew how it would look if the detectives found us. We were near the scene of a death, although the doctor had said that the poison had been administered sometime earlier.

Several sets of footsteps went past us, and Carl was just about to open the door when we heard the heavy footsteps of the detectives. As they passed us, we heard everything they said.

"He didn't actually say Daphne Delamare killed him," Clyde pointed out. "He just said she *did it*. That could mean anything, and it will seem that way to a jury."

"She certainly had the opportunity, and the motive as well," Rieker said. The two of them had paused quite close to the door, as we were able to hear them easily.

"I'm sure the doctor's right, but we'll need to do a bit more digging into these death cap mushrooms. Find out the shortest time someone could die after administration. This makes things more difficult now, given that it was possibly administered well before the party. If we can't pinpoint the time of the poison's administration, that will make it a very difficult case to solve."

Rieker was the next to speak. "I feel sorry for Ms Myers because of that dreadful newspaper article this morning. The whole town will blame her. She will probably go broke. Everyone will think her chocolates were poisoned."

"True, but that's not our responsibility," Clyde said brusquely. "Our duty is to solve this murder, but it seems as if we have a plethora of suspects, and right now, Daphne Delamare is looking like the main person of interest."

"And there's no chance of accidental ingestion?" Rieker asked. "I googled death cap mushrooms, and they can be mistaken for common mushrooms."

Clyde made a strange sound at the back of his throat. "No, you heard what Dr Marshall said last night. He said the victim ingested a huge amount and on a continual basis. Find out if he cooked his own meals, and arrange for his place to be searched right now. I shouldn't think anyone will force us to get a search warrant. If Dorothy Delamare cooked his meals, then the finger is pointing firmly at her."

They said more, but they had started walking again, and we couldn't hear. After what seemed an age, we emerged from the cupboard, none the worse for wear. We walked briskly back through the corridors, avoiding eye contact with all the nurses, who were busily going about their own business.

"Carl, I'm done for," I wailed, as soon as we were outside. "Did you hear what they said? They said I was going to go broke!"

"Calm your farm, Narel," Carl said. "They were talking idle nonsense."

I clutched my throat. "Do you really think so?"

"No. They probably meant it." He held up both hands to placate me and then unlocked his car. "Narel, I hate to admit when you're right, but it looks as though we are going to have to solve this murder by ourselves. One thing is sure; Daphne Delamare didn't do it."

"How do you know that?"

Carl didn't answer, but jumped in his car. I followed suit. When we had buckled up, Carl reversed the car, keeping his eyes firmly on his reversing camera. "Why do people walk behind a reversing car?" Carl said crossly.

I poked him in the ribs. "You haven't told me."

Carl shot a look at me. "Told you what?"

"You haven't told me why you think Daphne Delamare didn't do it."

"I don't *think* she didn't do it, I *know*. If she did poison him, why would she come to his retirement party and make a scene? Until that point, probably no one knew she was having an affair with him, but now everyone does. Not only that, but now everyone knows that she had a big argument with him."

"Oh, that makes sense." I thought on it some more. "Actually, it doesn't make sense."

Carl swore at the hat driver in front of us. In Australian country towns, *hat driver* is the term used to refer to slow-driving farmers who wear big hats while driving erratically. Most of the time, hat drivers drive at a fraction of the speed limit and invariably never indicate before or during turning, although some indicate randomly a few minutes after turning. They are also likely to slam on the brakes for no reason. This hat driver was doing ten kilometres in a fifty kilometre zone. Carl finally managed to pass the hat driver, who sped up and swerved into our lane as Carl did so.

"What did you say, Narel?" He made a rude sign at the hat driver, who waved happily back.

I was still clutching my seat. My accident had left me terrified of cars. In fact, I still hadn't bought my own car. I thought I should get used to being a passenger first. "I said it didn't make sense. I mean, she could well be the murderer, because she might have staged that scene to make everyone think she only found out that night that he was cheating on her. That would absolve her from blame, don't you see?" Carl didn't answer, so I continued. "We overheard the detectives and the doctor saying that Stan was actually poisoned several days ago. That is, that he would have eaten the first lot of death cap mushrooms then, a few days ago. Do you see what I mean?"

Carl shook his head. "Not really."

I sighed. "Okay. The murderer poisoned Stan Wellings several days ago. Sure, they could have kept poisoning him, but they first poisoned him several days ago. Correct?"

Carl nodded.

"What if Daphne Delamare knew he was having an affair all along and poisoned him several days ago, but staged that scene last night to make it look as though she had only just found out that he was having an affair. That was a big public scene, so everyone present would think that she had only just discovered it. Since the medical evidence is that he was poisoned several days earlier, that would let her off the hook. What if it was all a big act on her part?"

Carl was silent for a few moments. "I see where you're going with it, Narel, but it sounds far too complicated to me."

"It would be clever of her though, wouldn't it?"

"If she was the murderer, then it would be very clever of her, I suppose," Carl conceded. "Narel, you need to come to my place and I'll make you some lunch. Then we can go over all the suspects. We need to solve this case as soon as possible."

That made me feel better. We had overheard the police saying it was a very difficult case, and while I was sure they would solve it in the end, I still wanted my chocolate shop to be successful by the time they did.

CHAPTER 8

If I had to describe Carl's house in one word, it would be 'white.' The walls were white; the floors were white; the kitchen was white; even Carl's fancy cat, the former show champion, Louis the Fourteenth, was white. Louis the Fourteenth was as well-groomed as Carl's immaculate house was clean. There was not a single cat hair to be seen, quite a feat considering Louis the Fourteenth was a Persian.

It was then no surprise that Carl favoured whiteboards when figuring out a problem. Whiteboards were everywhere in the living room—propped against the walls, on whiteboard stands, on tables. The only colour I could see was the blue whiteboard marker.

Carl snatched up his whiteboard marker with delight. "Narel, we'll start with making lists of suspects, and then we will cross-reference them to motives. Do you think we should have a separate whiteboard for each suspect?"

"I'm not sure if you have enough whiteboards for that," I said, trying to conjure up a list of suspects in my mind.

Carl shook his whiteboard marker at me. "I know! We'll have a whiteboard for each of the main suspects, and then we will put everyone else, excluding ourselves, of course, on another whiteboard or two."

I agreed that that was a good idea. Carl wrote Daphne Delamare's name across the top of one whiteboard, and underlined it with a flourish.

"And don't forget we have to put The Purr-suader on another whiteboard," I said.

Carl pouted, but nevertheless did as I asked. He spun around, his marker in the air. "I suppose we should put Miriam Moreton, Stan's personal secretary, on a white-board by herself. She did seem to like him, but that could have been an act, and she did ask you to make the fly agaric mushrooms." He nodded furiously. "Clever. Yes, I could see why she did that. Very clever ordering fly agaric mushrooms and then poisoning them with death cap mushrooms."

"Well, we don't know if she actually did it, Carl," I said. "And if she did it, why wouldn't she ask me to make death cap mushroom chocolates?"

For some reason, Carl seemed to think that particularly funny. "Can you hear yourself, Narel? Why would anyone ask someone to make chocolate replicas of a deadly mushroom?"

I shook my finger at him. "I'll have you know, fly agaric mushrooms are very poisonous as well. They can be quite deadly, too."

Carl pursed his lips. "But they're so pretty," he protested.

I simply shrugged. Pursuing this line of conversation

wasn't going to get me anywhere. "Who else can we have as suspects?" I asked him.

Carl fetched another whiteboard stand and placed a bulky whiteboard on it. "Mick Holder, the sheep shearer."

"Yes, because Stan wouldn't allow him to be with Minnie."

Carl shook his head. "No, Narel. Right now we're just thinking of suspects. We will get to motives later."

My stomach growled. "Didn't you mention lunch, Carl?"

"Yes, you can have lunch as your reward, once we get all the suspects written on the whiteboards. I'm adding Minnie to this whiteboard, and who else is there?"

"Craig Cooper, the colleague," I said suddenly. "He certainly didn't like Stan."

Carl wrote Craig's name on another whiteboard, and then placed all the whiteboards in a line. He turned to me and ticked off the suspects on his fingers. "Dorothy Delamare, The Purr-suader, Craig, Minnie, Mick. Is that all?" He seemed disappointed.

"I think so. I'll think better on a full stomach," I said pointedly.

"All right, all right. Let's go into the kitchen."

The kitchen, of course, was as immaculate as the rest of Carl's house. I was surprised he even cooked in there. Still, I knew he was one of those people who cleaned up after every part of the cooking process. "How about a nice healthy salad, Narel?"

I groaned. "Is there dessert?"

Carl pouted. "If you eat all your salad, maybe I will let you have some chocolate ice cream."

"Can I have some chocolates on top of it?"

Carl looked quite put out. He bent down to stroke Louis the Fourteenth who was rubbing between his legs, purring loudly. "It depends on how much salad you eat."

"But Carl, if I've told you once, I've told you a thousand times, I can't eat much at once. You know, from what they had to do to my insides with all my terrible injuries. That's why I can't put on weight—well, it's one of the ghastly medical reasons, anyway."

Carl brandished a lettuce leaf. "If you eat a small amount of salad, then I will give you a small amount of chocolate ice cream with one chocolate on the top. Deal?"

I had to admit defeat. "All right, then," I said sadly.

"I'm sure Porridge wants his women fit and healthy," Carl said archly.

"Carl, please call him Tom, not Borage, or Porridge for that matter. Anyway, I'm not Tom's *woman,* and I *am* working on getting myself fit and healthy."

Carl simply added a sliced tomato to my salad bowl by way of response.

Something suddenly occurred to me. I slapped myself on the side of my head. "Why didn't I think of that before?" I pulled my phone from my pocket and googled images of death cap mushrooms.

Carl abandoned his addition of more vegetables to my plate and came to look over my shoulder. "What are you doing?"

"I'm seeing what death cap mushrooms actually look like. I'm wondering if that was what I saw on top of the fly agaric." I slid my thumb across the screen and then pointed. "Yes, it looked exactly like one of those young ones. You know, a small one would look like a marshmallow."

"But surely he'd know if he ate a mushroom?" Carl asked in a bewildered tone. "He'd know it wasn't a marshmallow, or a chocolate for that matter. Still, perhaps he thought it was a type of avant-garde chocolate. Yes, that must have been it." He nodded slowly.

"Hang on a minute." I scrolled down to read the description of death cap mushrooms. "It says here that they taste delicious."

Carl pulled a face. "Maybe so, but they wouldn't taste like chocolate."

"I had other textures in there as well," I reminded him. "The stems were a type of meringue. Besides, he shoved the chocolates in his face so fast that he wouldn't have had a clue what he was tasting."

Carl pushed the salad bowl across the table to me. I regarded it with caution. Lettuce? Why would anyone eat lettuce? "You know, Carl, I've just had a brilliant business idea. What if I make chocolate-coated vegetables?"

Carl stared at me as if I had gone mad. Finally, he spoke. "You're joking, right? On second thoughts, don't answer that. Hurry up and eat your salad if you want some ice cream."

"I'm not a child," I protested, but I did as he asked. It was worth the torture of eating the salad to get to the delicious chocolate ice cream with the chocolate on top. "Can I have another chocolate, Carl?"

Carl shook his head. "Narel, you keep telling me you can't eat much, but you've eaten a whole salad, a small bowl of chocolate ice cream, and one chocolate."

"There wasn't much chocolate," I said plaintively.

Carl ignored me. "Back to work!" He marched back into the living room, with me following behind. "Now we have to look at motives. Let's look at the obvious motives first. Minnie's motive was that her father wouldn't let her see Mick."

"That's a pretty lame motive," I said. "Lots of parents don't let their daughters see guys, and the daughters don't murder them for that."

Carl held up a hand in protest. "I said we would write the motives, and we can decide later whether they are bad or good motives. For now, we just write the motives."

"Okay."

Carl was on a roll. "And Mick's motive was that Stan wouldn't let him see Minnie. What was Craig's motive again?"

I bit my lip. "I don't really know, but Craig didn't like Stan. He made disparaging remarks about him."

Carl seemed pleased by that. "I'll just write that he didn't like him, but we need to do some more digging on that one. They both worked at the same ad agency, so they were competitors. There was probably some dirty dealing on Stan's part and we'll have to find out what it was."

"And we have to see if The Purr-suader was in fact married to Stan's wife, before she was Stan's wife, I mean," I added.

Carl wrote that across the board. "And Daphne Delamare. Her motive is obvious. She found out that Stan was having an affair with Peaches." His hand flew to his mouth. "I forgot Peaches!"

"So did I." I wondered how anyone could possibly forget Peaches. The image of the woman's impossibly stretched face and incredibly huge lips flashed before me. Carl fetched another stand and neatly placed a whiteboard on top. He wrote Peaches' name with a flourish and underlined it three times. "I'm going to write that Peaches had a possible motive, namely, that she found out that Stan was cheating on her with other women, at least with Daphne, the housekeeper," Carl said.

I pointed to one of the blank whiteboards. "Just write Stan's colleagues there. Miriam said that Stan wasn't well liked, so there must have been other people in the office who had a grudge against him."

"Which brings us to Miriam," Carl said. "I wonder what motive she had, if any."

I stretched back on the sofa and groaned. "There are just too many suspects. Too many suspects, Carl, and not enough clues."

"That's because we haven't begun digging yet," Carl said, undaunted. "How about we invite The Purr-suader back to your place to work on Mongrel? We can pump him for information."

"I doubt he'll come back," I said. "You saw what happened to him."

"I'm sure he didn't need too many stitches," Carl said. "Besides, he left with all his fingers intact—at least I think he did. It won't hurt to ask him. Anyway, I'll bet his professional pride is involved."

I leant forward. "Maybe you're right. Now let's look at opportunity. Daphne was obviously the one with the most opportunity, and possibly Peaches, too. And Minnie. If the doctor was right about Stan's initial poisoning occurring a few days ago, then anyone could have slipped him poisoned mushrooms at his home."

"But if the doctor was wrong and he was given a massive dose that night, then The Purr-suader had the opportunity, because he was alone in your kitchen and he was overly interested in your chocolates."

"Of course he was interested in my chocolates," I said, somewhat put out. "Isn't everyone?"

Carl raised one perfectly shaped eyebrow. "At this stage, we don't know that Mick had the opportunity. Miriam had the opportunity to slip him poisoned mushrooms at work, and so did Craig for that matter. So far, the only one who doesn't have the opportunity—as far as we know—is Mick."

"Oh great!" I said sarcastically. "So many suspects, all with motives, and most of them had the opportunity. How on earth are we ever going to solve this crime, Carl?"

Carl smiled enigmatically. "The journey of a thousand miles begins with the first step. We'll start investigating these people one by one. I'm sure our investigations will turn up something. You wait and see, Narel."

As if on cue, Louis the Fourteenth deigned to stretch out one long white paw and tap my knee.

CHAPTER 9

"I've had a brainwave," Carl announced proudly. He studied the whiteboards a little longer, and then swung around to me, his hands in the air. "We just need the guest list."

I thought that over for a moment. "So we can find some other suspects?"

Carl nodded enthusiastically. "Yes, so we will know everyone who was there. That will give us all the suspects."

"It might not. Don't forget that Stan was poisoned days earlier," I reminded him.

Carl wagged his finger at me. "Yes, but what you're forgetting is that the doctor said he likely had a massive dose the night of his retirement party. That meant it had to be someone present."

I continue to disagree, much to Carl's chagrin. "Someone didn't have to be physically present; they simply had to poison the fly agaric chocolates, and if it was The Purr-suader, then he would have done it at my place."

Carl sighed dramatically. "Oh Narel, you've become so precise lately. Who else had access to the chocolates before the event?" Without waiting for me to answer, he said, "Me, you, and The Purr-suader. Of course, Mongrel had access too, but I don't think we can blame him this time."

"Okay, so you're saying that the murder suspects can only consist of the people on the guest list plus The Purr-suader?"

Carl's eyes lit up. "Exactly! So now all we have to do is get the guest list."

"How are we going to do that?" I asked him.

"Just ask Miriam for it, of course."

"Are you going to ask her?" I asked hopefully.

"No, of course not." Carl pulled a face. "She paid you to make the chocolates, not me."

I rubbed my temples. "What reason will I give her for asking for the guest list? I can't tell her the truth. I can't say that we're investigating the murder because we think my shop will go broke by the time the police get around to solving it. We can't tell her that she's a suspect, and ask her to hand us the guest list so we can add the people on to one of your whiteboards."

"You're making it sound worse than it really is," Carl said. "Just ask for the guest list."

"I can't," I protested. "She'll ask me what I want it for."

"We'll make up something," Carl said, unhelpfully.

"Yes, let's both make up something now so we'll have an excuse to tell her."

Carl threw himself on the sofa. After a few minutes of silence, he said, "I haven't thought of anything."

"Carl, I am definitely not asking her for the guest list, unless you can come up with a solid excuse."

Carl pouted. "Okay then, but you have to help me."

"Okay." For the next few minutes we brainstormed, but still couldn't come up with anything. "What if I said I wanted the guest list so I could send everyone on it a card of condolences," I said.

Carl shook his head. "I don't think that would work."

"Why not? I think it's a good idea."

Carl shook his head again. "I know! How about we say we found a valuable piece of jewellery that had fallen into the chocolate fountain, and when you cleaned out the chocolate fountain, you found it. We need the guest list so we can contact everyone in turn."

It didn't sound such a good idea at first, but the more I thought about it, the more attractive it seemed. "Okay, I suppose we haven't come up with anything better, though I did like the idea of condolence cards."

"Come on, Narel. Grab your purse and let's get out of here."

I stood up. "Where are we going?"

"To get that guest list, of course."

"But Carl, it's Saturday afternoon. Miriam won't be at the office."

Carl did not seem put out. "No matter. It's a valuable piece of jewellery, isn't it?"

"But she'll be devastated that Stan has just died. We can't upset her at a time like this."

"Don't forget, she could be the murderer. It will give us

an opportunity to see if she's acting or if she is genuinely upset."

I thought it was a bad idea, a really bad idea, but I knew I wouldn't be able to talk Carl out of it. I sighed and followed him to his car. When he didn't drive off, but just sat there tapping away at his phone, I asked him, "What are you doing?"

"Finding out where she lives, of course."

Five minutes later, we pulled up outside Miriam's house. It was a new villa, all white brick and white hardiplank, one of five villas backing onto a bushland reserve. As we walked up to her doorway, I clutched Carl's arm. "Are you sure we should do this? What if she doesn't know that Stan is already dead? What if the police haven't released the information yet?"

"Oh Narel, you worry too much. Leave it to me. I'll do all the talking."

That sounded good to me, although I knew Carl wasn't always tactful. Carl knocked on the door, and it was with mixed feelings that I heard someone approach. Miriam opened the door, and it was clear she had been crying. At once, I figured she couldn't be the murderer. After all, she didn't know we were coming, so there was no point faking red eyes—unless, of course, she was the murderer and was overcome with remorse.

She looked quite shocked to see us both standing there. "Narel!"

"Hello." I waited for Carl to start speaking, but he stood there, speechless, so I elbowed him in the ribs. He still didn't speak, so I said, "Carl has something to say."

Carl cleared his throat. "We're sorry to hear about Stan."

Miriam's eyes scrunched and she covered her face with the tissue for a few moments. Carl pushed on. "We need your guest list, the guest list for the party last night."

Miriam pulled the tissue away from her face and looked surprised. "Whatever for?"

I decided to intervene, given that Carl wasn't doing a good job. "I'm so terribly sorry to bother you at a time like this," I began, "but when I was cleaning the chocolate fountain last night, I found a very valuable piece of jewellery that must've dropped inside. I mentioned it to the police, but they said they would call me if anyone came forward for it. No one has as yet, and I didn't want to bother the police at such a terrible time as this, given that, well you know..." My voice trailed away.

Miriam covered her face once more with the tissue. I pushed on. "If you wouldn't mind giving us the guest list, I can contact each person in turn and find out who owns the jewellery."

To my great surprise, that seemed to work. Miriam removed the tissue from her face and looked at us hesitantly. "Would you like to come in?"

Carl made to step forward, but I grabbed him by his arm. "No, no, thank you. We're so terribly sorry to bother you at this time, but we thought that whoever lost it must be quite distraught, and we also wanted to come and say how terribly sorry we were."

Miriam nodded wordlessly and disappeared. The door was only partially open so we couldn't see inside her house. It was one of those doors with narrow horizontal glass panels; only the glass panels were frosted. She soon returned and handed me a list. "If anyone tells me that they lost it, can I tell them to contact you directly?"

"Of course, that would be great," I said, feeling a little guilty about telling such an outrageous lie.

We both murmured our condolences once more and then hightailed it back to Carl's car.

Unfortunately, we were only halfway to the car when we met the detectives walking up the driveway. "Fancy seeing you two here," Detective Clyde said with barely veiled disgust. "I hope you're not interfering in this investigation."

"We were just coming to say how sorry we were to Miriam," I said. "She's a friend of mine, after all." That was an outrageous exaggeration, but the detectives had no way of knowing that.

"Sorry about what?" Clyde asked pointedly.

"About her boss's death, of course," I said.

"That hasn't been released to the media yet, Miss Myers," he snapped at me.

I gestured around me. "Bush telegraph," I said, referring to the Aussie expression about gossip spreading like wildfire in a small country town.

Clyde simply scowled and went on his way, while Detective Rieker afforded Carl a small smile.

When we were safely in the car, Carl laughed. "That went well, didn't it! Apart from running into those detectives. Of all the timing! Of course, I'm not complaining about running into Detective Rieker."

"It did go surprisingly well," I conceded. "I really didn't think she would give us the guest list. I didn't think she would believe such an outrageous lie. Actually, I was worried that she'd ask us what type of jewellery it was."

"People never ask in situations like that," Carl said with confidence.

"Whyever not?"

Carl started the engine and pulled onto the road. "If we actually had found a valuable piece of jewellery, we would not describe it to anyone. Only the owner would be able to describe it, and that way, we would know it was them. Make sense?"

I nodded. "I suppose." I looked through the guest list. "Oh Carl, there are so many people here. How will we go through all of them?"

"One by one," Carl said. "Do you know, something's been bothering me. Okay, we know that the murderer poisoned Stan at his house several days ago."

I interrupted him. "It mightn't have been at his house. He could have been visiting someone else for dinner."

Carl waved a hand at me in dismissal. "Yes, yes, whatever. Forget that. My point is, someone poisoned Stan several days ago and in large quantities. Right?"

I agreed.

"And they poisoned him again, according to that doctor, last night, at his office party. Right?"

"Yes, but I don't see where you're going with this."

"Don't you see, Narel? Anyone could have poisoned him at his house, or wherever, several days ago, but only those people on that list could have poisoned him that night."

"Or The Purr-suader," I reminded him.

Carl nodded. "Okay, leaving The Purr-suader aside for a moment, let's look at what we have so far. Someone poisoned Stan several days ago, possibly over a period of days, but the fact is that the doctor said from that moment on, Stan was going to die and couldn't be saved. So why did they poison him again last night? What I mean is, anyone could have poisoned him several days ago. For that, there would be way too many suspects and no one could pin it down, but the fact that he was poisoned last night meant it had to be someone who had access to the chocolates. That meant it had to be someone in the room."

"And The Purr-suader."

"And The Purr-suader," Carl said with a laugh. "Narel, has anyone told you that you're getting more annoying lately?" I gave him a playful slap on the arm. "But you don't seem to get what I mean. Someone poisoned him several days ago. Given that he didn't receive medical treatment at the time, he was a ticking time bomb. He couldn't be saved after that, so why would they poison him again last night? That meant that the murderer had to be someone who was in that room, someone with access to the chocolates. Leaving The Purr-suader aside for the moment, it had to be someone in that room. Why would they do that? That threw the suspicion onto a small amount of people."

"Are you saying it's pointing to The Purr-suader, then?"

Carl shrugged. "Perhaps, but not necessarily. I can see two possibilities. One is that it was The Purr-suader, and because he wasn't at the party, then it would have been a good idea on his part to make it look like it was someone at the party. The second possibility—well, the only other possibility—is that someone at the party poisoned Stan again for a very specific reason, and if we can find out what that reason was, then we will know who the murderer is."

My head was spinning by this point. I reached into my

purse and pulled out some chocolates, which I rapidly consumed.

"Narel, I thought you were trying to get healthy," Carl admonished me.

"Low blood sugar," I said, half believing it. "Where do we go from here?"

"I think we should start with The Purr-suader, if only to eliminate him."

"Carl, I forgot to ask you. Did you call Detective Rieker and tell him what Tom said about Peter Patterson being a possible connection with Stan Wellings?"

Carl nodded. "Yes, I did, but he didn't say anything. He gave nothing away, and that is why I have invited Peter to your place for dinner tonight."

CHAPTER 10

Luckily for me, Carl insisted on helping me prepare dinner for The Purr-suader. "I'm sure he doesn't want chocolates for the main course," Carl said.

"What's wrong with him?" I exclaimed.

"Sometimes I wonder about you, Narel." Carl strained the pasta in the sink. "I invited him to your place for dinner to pretend to make up for Mongrel attacking him."

"Yes, you've told me that several times already," I said. "But we're the clients, remember? We paid him—or rather *you* paid him—to help Mongrel with his aggression problems. He can't really charge someone to help with their cat's aggression problems and then expect sympathy when he's attacked."

Carl waved a hand at me. "No matter, it's all a pretence so we can see if he's the murderer."

Something occurred to me. "If he *is* the murderer, was it a good idea to invite him for dinner? What if he poisons us?"

Carl placed the saucepan on a stand. "If he did kill Stan Wellings, then I'm sure he had a motive for killing him, and him specifically. It's not as if he's a serial killer."

I wasn't so sure. "If he's the killer, then he's gone to a lot of trouble to poison the chocolates at my place. He must have done a lot of research. He must've found out that I was preparing the chocolates for the retirement party, and then come here offering to train Mongrel. Besides, doesn't it work a bit too much in his favour that I have an aggressive cat? That seems like far too much of a coincidence."

Carl bit his lip. "Maybe you're right. Maybe he isn't the murderer, but we need to find out if we can exclude him. He's the only fly in the ointment, so to speak. If we can rule him out, then we're a lot closer to figuring out who the murderer really was, because as I said earlier, the murderer had a good reason to give Stan a second dose of poison at that time. Oh gosh, is that him already? He's early. Be on your guard, Narel."

"You, too." I walked over to the door, and sure enough, The Purr-suader was standing there, both hands wrapped in bandages. I wondered how he would be able to eat. Maybe we should have made soup and given him a straw. "Lovely to see you, Peter." I almost went to shake his hand, and then realised that was a bad idea. "Please come in."

The Purr-suader looked around the door nervously. "Where's your cat?"

I pointed to the carrier basket. "He was sitting at the kitchen table, but when he heard a knock on the door, he ran into his basket. He's not very sociable."

"You're telling me!" The Purr-suader snapped, but then

quickly replaced his expression with what I judged to be a fake smile. "Do you want your money back?"

I hurried to reassure him. "No, no, not at all! I'm so sorry about Mongrel attacking you. We've invited you to dinner to try to make up for it."

"That's very kind of you," he said, eyeing Mongrel's basket nervously. For a famous Cat Whisperer, I didn't think he was doing very well.

"Please have a seat. Would you like some wine?"

"Yes, please." He was still staring fixedly at Mongrel's basket. I had placed lavender scented candles around the room, but perhaps the soothing effect only worked on cats, because it certainly wasn't working on The Purrsuader.

"Oh you'll be fine," I said. "He only reacts to rope."

Carl sailed into the room. "Which is why we enlisted your services in the first place." He shot the man a sickly sweet smile after he said it. "Cheese and dip?" He placed a cheese platter on the coffee table in front of Peter.

"I'm sorry, what would you like to drink?" I asked him. "Red, white, or bubbly?"

"Bubbly would be good."

"Dry? Or I have a bubbly Moscato?"

"Dry, please." Peter seemed to be starting to relax, and leant back in his seat.

"I'll get it." Carl disappeared from the room, and I heard a popping sound. There were two soft armchairs opposite the sofa on which Peter was sitting, and I sat in the one to his right. An awkward silence descended, and I wondered how to start the conversation. "How are your hands?" I asked him. "Will you be able to eat?"

Peter's body stiffened. "Yes, I'm left-handed actually,

and it's the right hand that is more affected. The fingers on my left hand are bandaged separately."

"Oh, so they are!" The atmosphere was decidedly tense now, and I wished I hadn't asked about his hands. I hoped Carl would get some conversation going when he returned with the bubbly.

Carl sailed into the room, holding three flutes of bubbly. He set them all down on the coffee table. "Drink up!" He sat in the other armchair.

"You have a nice place here, Narel," Peter said, obviously feeling uncomfortable.

Carl waved his hand at him. "Oh, puh-lease! It's a dump. Narel is going to sell it soon and buy a better place, isn't that right, Narel?"

I nodded, wondering how we were going to turn the conversation around to the matter of Stan Wellings' murder. I thought I might as well get right to it. "Did you hear what happened last night?"

The expression on Peter's face didn't change. "No?"

"Remember those chocolates I showed you? I said we were going to an office retirement party last night?"

Peter nodded.

"The man there was murdered."

Peter's jaw dropped open. I judged it to be a genuine reaction, but then again, I could be wrong. "You're kidding!" he said. "Murdered? Right there, in front of everyone?"

"He was poisoned," Carl said. "You might know the man anyway, Stan Wellings."

Peter jumped so much that his bubbly spilt and ran down his bandages and onto his leg. I hurried out of the room to fetch something to mop it up. When I returned to the room, Peter was sitting there, his jaw working up and down. All the colour had drained from his face. "Stan Wellings," he repeated. "Do the police know who did it?"

I shook my head. "No. I'm sorry, Peter, I didn't realise you knew him. I would have broken the news more gently. You look quite upset. Was he a good friend of yours?" I said.

Peter took the offered kitchen wipe and mopped his leg and his bandaged hand. He then handed it to Carl who all but ran from the room and came back in double quick time. "Yes, I knew him very well years ago. I imagine he has a lot of enemies, so I'm sure it'll make it hard for the police to discover who murdered him."

"What do you mean?" Carl asked innocently.

"Stan is, or rather was, crooked. He was a nasty piece of work. He trampled anyone who got in his way. I suppose he could have changed in the years since I knew him, but then they say that a leopard never changes its spots."

I offered Peter the cheese platter, but he shook his head. "Go on," I said. "How did you know Stan? I must say, I only met him last night, but I was chatting to one of his colleagues and he didn't have a good word to say about him, either. Even his personal secretary said he had a lot of enemies."

Peter nodded. "It sounds like he hasn't changed, then. I'm not surprised."

"So how did you know him, Peter?" I tried not to look too interested as I said it. I took a large sip of wine in an attempt to look nonchalant but I somehow managed to pour it down the side of my face, missing my mouth completely. I quickly wiped my face, hoping Peter hadn't noticed.

"We actually worked in the same advertising agency in Sydney, back in the day," Peter said. "I know it's a competitive business, but he did all sorts of nasty things."

"Like what?" Carl asked him.

"Just the usual sort of office politics, only in his case, it was worse. In fact, I'm pretty sure he blackmailed a few people. He also lied to the boss about what other people were doing. I mean, blatant lies. He got at least one guy sacked that I know of. He was just a thoroughly nasty human being."

"That's awful," I said after a long interval, when it became clear he wasn't going to add anything. "I'll just check on the dinner."

Carl stood up. "I'll help you."

"It's clear that this guy is the one Tom heard about, for sure and certain," Carl whispered to me. "Obviously the police haven't been to see him yet, because he was awfully shocked when you told him that Stan died. Either that, or he's a good actor. You know, I should check whether he has a theatre background."

I ignored the latter remark. "Yes, Peter must be the one Tom told me about. Peter didn't say that Stan stole his wife, but that's probably something too personal to tell strangers."

"We could always tell him that if he doesn't confess, we'll throw a piece of rope on him and let Mongrel out of his basket."

I eyed Carl warily. "Carl, sometimes I don't know whether you're joking."

Carl plastered an innocent look on his face. "Would you like to tell Peter that dinner is ready?"

I duly summoned Peter to the table. Carl was part way through serving us all, when Peter let out a bloodcurdling shriek. "Oh my goodness, what is it?" Carl said. "I nearly dropped this food all over the floor."

Peter seemed unable to speak, because he merely pointed. Mongrel had left his basket and was now sitting at the end of the table in his usual position, his paws resting on top of the table. "Oh, how cute," I said. "Mongrel must like you after all, Peter. He only comes out of his basket when he's comfortable with someone."

"Or if he's going to attack someone," Carl added, rather unhelpfully.

I glared at Carl. "He only comes out to sit at the table when he's happy," I reiterated.

Peter appeared to be shaking, but managed to speak. "He's staring straight at me."

"That means he likes you," I said. "Isn't that right Carl?" I glared at Carl and raised my eyebrows.

"Yes, that's right." Carl's tone was less than convincing, but I was telling the truth. If Mongrel had wanted to attack Peter, he would have done so already, but I thought I perhaps should not point that out. And if Mongrel liked Peter, that meant Peter couldn't be the murderer.

"Please eat up," Carl said to Peter. "You haven't started eating."

Peter appeared to be frozen to the spot. "I don't want to make any sudden moves."

"Oh, you're perfectly all right," I assured him. "He only attacks people if they have a piece of rope."

"And murderers," Carl added.

"Murderers?" Peter repeated in rather a high voice.

"Yes, he's attacked two murderers in the past."

Carl nodded vigorously. "Yes, that's right. He doesn't like murderers."

Peter appeared to be thinking that over, but gingerly reached for his fork and ever so slowly started to eat his food. I fully expected him to ask how Mongrel had come to meet murderers, but he didn't. All the time, he didn't take his eyes off Mongrel, not even for a second.

Peter excused himself after finishing his pasta, thanking us very much for our hospitality but saying he needed to go home to bed and take painkillers. He couldn't get out of the house fast enough. I was shocked that he didn't want dessert, given that it was a white chocolate fudge brownie cheesecake with chocolate custard. Oh well, there's no accounting for taste.

"That didn't go very well," Carl said only seconds after I shut the door.

"Shush, he'll hear you."

"He won't know what I'm talking about," Carl continued in the same loud tone,

I hurried back to the kitchen. "Oh well, we can't waste this dessert. Now there's more for us. Why did you think it didn't go very well? I thought it went very well indeed."

"We didn't really get any information out of him."

I spooned half the white chocolate fudge brownie cheesecake into a bowl for Carl and the remainder into a bowl for me. I poured the chocolate custard over the top. Mongrel was still sitting at the edge of the table, so I put some little treats in front of him. He was developing good table manners, in the sense that he allowed me to remove my hand before he viciously attacked the treats and gobbled them up. "To the contrary, we did. We know he's the guy that Tom mentioned, and he genuinely seemed surprised when he heard that Stan Wellings was dead. More to the point, Mongrel didn't attack him."

"Mongrel would have attacked him if there was any rope on him."

"True, but you're missing the point. Mongrel only comes out of his basket near people he likes, and he was sitting in the chair with his paws on the table directly opposite Peter."

"Narel, you're right! Mongrel wouldn't be so comfortable around Peter if he knew he was a murderer. Cats can sense these things."

"I'm sure Mongrel can sense things like that," I said with confidence. "Carl, would you think I was silly if we crossed The Purr-suader's name off our list of suspects?"

"I won't cross him right off, Narel, but I will put him on the bottom of the list. Actually, I'll remove him from the main list and put him on the secondary list. And tomorrow, we investigate someone who is near the top of our list, namely, Mick."

"But it's a Sunday," I protested. "I like to sleep in on Sundays. It's the one day of the week when I can sleep in. I don't use my alarm on Sundays."

"You can sleep in if you want, Narel. What I have in mind starts late morning."

"I'm not going to his house, Carl," I said firmly. "I felt awful going to Miriam's house. I simply can't go to Mick's house."

Carl smiled. "Mick will be at the local rugby game tomorrow. We'll just happen to turn up and pretend we're there to support the local team. I even have a couple of old team scarves."

"Where did you get those?"

Carl flushed red and waved his finger at me. "Ask me no questions and I'll tell you no lies. Just be ready by ten."

I sighed. I wasn't into rugby, not at all.

CHAPTER 11

I watched as Tom busied himself in the kitchen, making us a breakfast of coffee, chocolate, and toast. A lock of golden hair kept falling into his eyes, and he smelt like fresh laundry, while the morning sun streamed in through the window, and birds chirped outside. It was such a nice morning, I didn't think of murder. Not even once.

"Breakfast is up." Tom set our plates down at the table. I picked up a slice of toast and sat down, while Tom stood behind me, giving my shoulders a rub.

"Such good service," I told him. "Will this cost me extra?"

"I don't know," Tom said. "I just work here."

And then I woke up.

It took me a moment or two to realise that I was in my own bed, and that I had been dreaming. I reached out to look at my phone. It was only seven. I realised then that it was Sunday morning, and I usually slept until eight on Sunday mornings. I tried to snuggle back under the covers and resume my dream, but gave up after a few minutes. It had been such a lovely dream, too.

I struggled out of bed and screamed when my foot brushed something furry. I looked down to see Mongrel sitting there. "Good morning, Mongrel," I said. "I'll have a shower and then fix you some breakfast."

Mongrel tilted his head to one side, and then stalked off, obviously affronted that I wasn't putting his needs first.

It wasn't until after I had a shower, fed Mongrel, and had several cups of coffee that I started to wake up. I expect the strain of worrying about the future of my chocolate shop had taken its toll on me. Hopefully, I would find out some more information today from Mick Holder at the rugby game. I certainly hoped Carl had a plan for extracting the information, because I sure didn't.

Carl had said he would collect me at nine, and he was right on time. I opened the door. I was surprised to see him dressed informally, and looking somewhat rugged—if anyone could ever call Carl rugged. "Dressed for the occasion, I see?"

Carl looked down at himself ruefully. "I'm trying to blend into the crowd," he said.

I didn't see how Carl could ever blend into a crowd, let alone a crowd at a rugby league game, but I knew better than to comment. "Good idea," I said wisely. "Do you have a plan for questioning Mick?"

"We'll just play it by ear."

I groaned. "You keep saying that."

"Exactly. And it's worked out so far, hasn't it?"

I had to admit that it had, although it had given me several tense moments. "When do we leave?"

"Now."

I looked at the time on my phone. "Already? But the game doesn't start until ten."

Carl nodded. "That's right. The game starts at ten, and then there will be lots of screaming, swearing, and drinking, and I suspect Mick will get drunker and drunker as the game goes on. The only chances of speaking to him are before the game, after the game, and at half time, but he'll probably be too drunk by half time."

I shrugged. "I see what you mean." I looked down to see Mongrel looking up at us.

"What does he want?" Carl asked nervously.

"I think he wants a pat."

Carl pulled a face. "You don't pat cats; you pat dogs. You stroke cats."

"All right then, Carl, you stroke Mongrel."

Carl put his hands behind his back. "No way! You stroke him, Narel."

As there wasn't any rope in sight, I bravely reached down and gave Mongrel's back a quick stroke. He purred and arched his back.

Carl clutched my arm. "What's that sound? Thunder?"

I laughed. "Mongrel's purring."

Carl looked doubtful. "Are you sure?"

I briefly stroked Mongrel again, and the purring got louder. "See, he likes it!"

"Are you sure he's not growling at you?"

"Of course not, Carl. You try."

Carl snatched his phone from his manbag and looked at the screen. "Oh goodness, is that the time? Let's go!" He was out of the door before I could speak.

I gave Mongrel another little stroke and then hurried after Carl.

It didn't take us long to reach the football field. In fact, it didn't take us long to go anywhere in this small town. There were lots of dirty utes parked all in a row, and some had cattle dogs tied up in the back. Luckily, those utes were parked in the shade. Men in old faded jeans and flannelette shirts wandered around. They were clutching cans of beer and swiping at flies, and were followed by red or black and tan kelpies and red or blue cattle dogs.

The home side fans were decked out in blue and white football scarves. I knew that was the home side because Carl and I were wearing the same scarves. The other side's fans were wearing scarves in stripes of the most hideous shades of brown and yellow imaginable. The colour reminded me of babies, and I don't mean their cute faces.

Carl nudged me. "Is that Mick? That man with a red kelpie standing next to him?"

I squinted and then shielded my eyes from the sun. "I think so, but I only saw him that night." I swatted at a dozen flies buzzing around my head.

"So did I," Carl reminded me. "He's wearing the home team's scarf."

"So is most of the crowd," I pointed out. "Oh my goodness, look at that." A brawl had broken out between someone wearing a blue and white scarf and someone wearing the hideously coloured scarf. They were pushing and shoving each other, but hadn't actually started punching each other yet. However, the string of obscenities they were screaming made my ears burn. A crowd gathered around them and egged them on, but before it could escalate, their mates intervened and pulled them apart.

"Follow me," Carl said as he took off towards the fight. "Let's speak to Mick." I hurried after him.

"Hello, Mick," Carl said. "It is Mick, isn't it? Do you remember me?"

Mick swallowed some beer before answering. "Do I know you?" His tone wasn't hostile, just surprised.

"We haven't met. I'm Carl, and this is my friend, Narel. We were at the dinner on Friday night. Narel made the chocolates."

Mick looked at me appraisingly. "Oh yes, you were in the paper."

"I didn't kill him!" I said, and then regretted the words as soon as they were out of my mouth.

To my relief, Mick laughed. "I'm sure you didn't. I'm sure you didn't know him well enough to kill him."

I didn't know how to respond to that, so simply said, "No. I never actually met him. It was his secretary, Miriam Moreton, who ordered the chocolates for him. Anyway, your girlfriend must be upset."

"My girlfriend?"

I was puzzled. "Yes, Minnie."

Mick took a large gulp of beer. "She's not my girlfriend."

"Oh, I'm terribly sorry," I said. "I thought…"

Mick interrupted me. "We were kind of dating a while back, but her father didn't approve of us, so we both moved on. I was surprised when she invited me to the party. I didn't realise it was his retirement party or I never would've gone. I just thought it was a bash." He bent down to rub his dog's head.

"A bash?"

Mick shot me an impatient look. "Yes, a bash, a party, you know?"

I didn't know, but I nodded. "That's strange."

"You're telling me! Perhaps she was hoping I'd punch the old fool."

"They didn't get on?"

Mick shrugged. He pulled his cigarette out of his mouth, and ground it under his foot. "Dunno. I just know he didn't want her dating the likes of me. He only wanted her to have those fancy boyfriends."

"She didn't have a boyfriend at the party," I said. "At least, I didn't notice one."

"Perhaps her father didn't approve of him, either. I know she's got one though, that's why we broke up."

"Did she invite you to the, um, bash in person?" I asked him.

He downed the rest of his beer, threw the can in a nearby garbage can—his aim was good—and then opened the beer in his other hand. "No, she texted me."

"How did the two of you meet?" Carl asked him.

"It was a B&S ball."

Carl was possibly afraid that I would ask what a B&S ball was, so he quickly said, "Oh yes, a Bachelors and Spinsters ball."

Mick nodded lazily. "Yeah, we were both blind drunk when we met, and then we woke up in my swag on the back of my ute the next morning. We figured we might as well start dating, since we'd both enjoyed ourselves as far as we could remember, you know?" He laughed.

Carl and I nodded.

"But we never really dated. We just had a few one

night stands here and there, I figure on her part just to annoy her father, and then she went off with some other guy, some Jake someone or other. Look, the game's about to start. I gotta go."

Mick and his dog abruptly took their leave, to join a crowd of people hanging over the fence and yelling verbal abuse at the referee before the game had even begun.

"We can go now, Narel," Carl said. "I don't think we'll get any more information out of him, not now that the game has started. What did you think of that?"

"I was surprised to hear that Mick wasn't Minnie's boyfriend," I said, shooing away a particularly persistent fly.

"Miss Myers!"

I swung around to see a camera in my face. It was the dreadful reporter, Graham Gibson. "Can I have a quote, Miss Myers? Do you deny that your chocolates were responsible for poisoning Stan Wellings?"

Carl grabbed my arm and pulled me away from the reporter. "Don't say a word," he said.

Graham Gibson followed us, hot on our heels as we made our way to Carl's car. I had awful mental images of how my surprised face would look on the front page of the next newspaper. Carl changed direction and took me into a crowd of local supporters. "That man's harassing us," he addressed the crowd at large. "He supports the other team, and he says they're going to thrash us today!"

At once, the angry throng crowded around the reporter, while Carl and I made our escape.

"Come on, let's go straight to my place so I can rearrange my whiteboards."

I shot a look over my shoulder, but the reporter hadn't

managed to break free of the crowd and follow us. "What did you have in mind?"

"I'm going to put Mick on the secondary suspects whiteboard and move Minnie to the top."

"And we have to track down this Jake."

"The plot thickens," Carl said with a laugh. "The question remains, why did Minnie invite Mick to her father's birthday party?"

"Maybe she didn't," I said.

Just then, we walked a little too close to a ute with a blue cattle dog tied in the back. The dog lunged for us angrily, with a menacing growl and a show of teeth. Carl and I jumped away. "Oh, that gave me such a fright," I said. "I didn't realise we were walking so close to those utes. Those dogs are so protective."

Carl patted his chest and then fanned his face with his hand. "I think that aged me one hundred years. Now, what were you saying?"

"I said maybe she *didn't* invite him. Mick said the invitation came by text. The housekeeper, Daphne, would have access to Minnie's phone, and she could have sent it. Minnie still lives in the family home, doesn't she?"

Carl nodded. "So they say. Yes, well I'll have to move Daphne to the top of the list."

"And whether Minnie or Daphne invited Mick, I'm guessing the reason was so that there'd be a big scene, so someone could poison the chocolates at that point. Mick was probably invited as a distraction."

We had reached Carl's car. He unlocked it, and we climbed inside. "If that's the case, then that rules out The Purr-suader."

I chewed the end of one fingernail. "You know, Carl, I

don't think we've made any progress, because something else is puzzling me. Daphne was also a distraction, wasn't she? Perhaps Daphne wasn't the one who invited Mick. Perhaps someone gained access to Minnie's phone and invited Mick solely to cause a distraction, and also told Daphne that Stan was cheating on her. That was another distraction. Daphne didn't have time to poison those chocolates. No, Carl, I think we should move Daphne to the bottom of your suspects list, not the top."

Carl rested his head on his steering wheel. "Oh my gosh, Narel. This case is just getting harder and harder."

CHAPTER 12

Carl, in his wisdom, had decided we should investigate Craig, and then Peaches. We had agreed that we should visit Craig at work, and I told Carl I would call him if the shop was quiet.

And sadly, that was the case—the shop was quiet, deathly quiet. Not even a passing tourist called in. Of course, Mondays were usually quiet, but not this bad. I was sure it was all because of the newspaper article. I popped another chocolate in my mouth and thought over the suspects. There were too many of them, and I was sure the police were having the same trouble. I was certain that an arrest wouldn't be anytime soon, and until that happened, I wouldn't attract any business to my shop. And the way country towns worked, if an arrest was a long time coming, it would be firmly entrenched in the locals' minds that I was the perpetrator, even if that was later proven not to be the case. That's just the way things worked around here.

I pulled out my phone and texted Carl to come and get

me, but I didn't press send. I looked out the door once more. There were people out and about, but they just weren't in my shop. I ate another chocolate and then pressed send.

Carl was there within minutes. "Business hasn't picked up?"

I shook my head, fighting back the tears. Carl gave me a quick hug. "Never mind, Narel, at least we can do something about it. You never know, Craig could prove the answer to the problem."

"You think he did it?" I asked him.

"Your guess is as good as mine," Carl said over his shoulder as I locked the door to the shop.

We were soon standing outside the advertising agency's office. A sudden wave of panic hit me. "Are you sure this is a good idea?"

Carl put his hand on the small of my back and propelled me forwards. "You always say that, Narel."

The impeccably groomed woman at the front desk looked up abruptly. "Can I help you?" Her tone was as sharp as her manner.

I nearly sneezed as a wave of expensive French perfume hit me. "Narel Myers and Carl Camden, here to see Craig Cooper."

She looked down her nose at me. "Do you have an appointment?"

"We were with Craig the other night when Stan was poisoned," Carl said in his no-nonsense voice. "Please call through to Craig now and tell him we're here."

Carl's air of authority worked, because the woman scowled but punched some buttons on her phone and spoke into it. "I have a Narel Myers and a Carl Camden here asking to see you. Are you available today?" She looked disappointed by his answer, and then said, "You may go up to his office now."

Carl took me by the arm and led the way. "How did you know where his office is?" I asked him.

"I looked at the emergency evacuation plan while she was calling Craig," he said smugly.

There was no personal secretary sitting outside Craig's room, just a big glass door with his name emblazoned across it in gold lettering. Carl knocked and a voice called out, "Come in."

When we walked in, Craig indicated the two seats across from his desk. We sat down.

"What can I do for you?" Craig asked us.

Carl and I had discussed a plan of action, and had decided we should come straight out with the truth. "I'm here about Stan's murder," I said, but Craig cut me off.

"I've already spoken to the police."

"But we want to do our own investigating, because…"

He interrupted me again. "You should leave it to the police."

"Look, Craig, you're a businessman. You should understand. I'm struggling to save my business. You must have seen my face plastered all over the local newspaper?"

Craig nodded, but thankfully remained silent on this occasion.

"The reason I'm here now is because I didn't have a single customer in my shop this morning. Not a single customer. And on Saturday, usually my busiest day, I only had tourists—not a single local. People think I killed Stan, and unless I can prove otherwise soon, that's the end of my business. I'm sure you can understand that. Can you please help me?"

Craig put down his pen. He leant back in his seat and appeared to be thinking it over. "All right, what do you want to know?"

"Anything you can tell us about Stan would be a help," I said.

"What sort of a man was he?" Carl asked him.

"Well, they say you shouldn't speak ill of the dead," Craig said and then began to do precisely that. "He was totally unscrupulous. I'm sure everyone in the office breathed a great sigh of relief when he said he was retiring, and truth be told, I'm sure some are secretly happy that he's dead." He held up his hands. "I know that's a terrible thing to say, but I'm telling you how it is."

"Can you give us any examples of what he did?" I asked him.

"Well, take what he did to me, for example. I was at the agency for a few years before he came, and as soon as he arrived, we didn't get on. In fact, he didn't get on with anyone here in the office. We used to have a master key so anyone could pop into anyone else's office if they needed something, but after he came, they had to do away with the master key. He let himself into people's rooms and spied on them."

"What did he do with the information specifically?" Carl asked him.

Craig was rapidly warming up to the subject. "Well, if he found any good ideas, he would pretend those ideas were his own. He came here to semi-retire, and he wasn't the boss here. The boss is in Sydney and rarely visits, usually only for meetings or if there is a huge contract. At any rate, the meetings are usually in Sydney. To give an example, there was a woman here who was quite successful, at least before Stan came. He stole her information, and sent insulting emails to her clients pretending they were from her. She got the sack. Everyone knew it was Stan, but no one could prove anything. He then took over that contract and presented those ideas as his own."

"It's a wonder she didn't murder him, then!" Carl exclaimed.

"She went to live in London as far as I know," Craig said, "but there's any number of people who suffered the same at Craig's hands, maybe even worse. Take me, for example."

"What did he do to you?" I asked him, now quite interested in the subject.

A look of distaste passed over his face. "I was already always very careful around Stan. I've been in this business a long time and I know how competitive it is. The two of us were always at each other's throats, but after he announced he was retiring, he came to my office one day and asked me out to the pub for a beer. We had quite a good chat over a few beers, and he apologised for everything he had done. He told me some big story about having a sad childhood and I believed him at the time. Call me stupid, I let down my guard around him." He went silent for a moment, staring off into the distance.

"What happened after that?" I asked, intrigued.

"He somehow got access to my laptop—don't ask me how. It was probably when I took a bathroom break at the pub that night. I had a big contract coming up. It was worth a considerable amount of money to me. Put it this way, I would have been able to pay off a big slab of my mortgage." He leant back in his chair and sighed before continuing. "Stan took that information, and gave it to my direct competitor in a rival firm. At the same time, he sent the company an email from my email address saying that I quit and calling them some rather unsavoury names."

"Was there any proof that he did it?" Carl asked him.

Craig shook his head. "If I'd known at the time, I probably could have had my laptop fingerprinted. Who knows? It was all over before I found out, and then there was nothing I could do about it. Of course, I challenged him about it to his face, and he outright denied it. I knew it was him. That was the sort of thing Stan did to everyone. If I didn't have family in this town, I would have gone to another agency in one of the capital cities just to get away from him."

"That's absolutely terrible," I said. "What a dreadful person. It seems like there must be dozens of people who wanted to murder him."

Craig nodded. "That's probably not an exaggeration."

"What about Mick Holder?" Carl asked him.

"Bogan Mick?" Craig cracked his knuckles. "Yes, he certainly pushed Stan's buttons. Stan wanted his daughter to marry some rich society snob."

"But surely Minnie and Mick weren't getting married?" I asked him.

"Oh no," Craig hurried to add. "I simply meant that Stan didn't like Minnie dating anyone at all, unless that person was someone rich and famous."

"So is Minnie actually dating Mick?" Carl said.

Craig shrugged. "No idea what Minnie is or isn't doing. Why else would she invite him to the party, if she wasn't dating him?"

I was about to say that Mick told us that they weren't dating, but Carl caught my eye and shook his head ever so slightly. "Does Minnie have any other boyfriends that you know of?" Carl asked him.

"I don't know. She didn't come to the office much."

"What was her relationship with her father like?" Carl continued.

"Fine, I suppose. She was spoilt rotten; he gave her anything she wanted. She's still living in his house, and she doesn't have a job. She's sponging off him. When the Sydney boss came, Stan always had a big dinner at his place for all of us, and Minnie was there then. And if you're wondering why we went, we had to go because the big boss was there. Stan's house was luxurious. It always annoyed me that he could have afforded to retire, but instead caused so much trouble for the rest of us who didn't have a fraction of his money. I suppose it was all a game to him."

"Is Minnie the sole heir to his money?" I asked him.

Craig twirled his pen between his fingers. "No idea. Peaches might get something. For all I know, Stan has a stack of illegitimate children who might get something, too."

"Can you think of anyone in particular who would have a motive for killing Stan?" I asked him. "I mean, Stan did terrible things to people over the years, but is there anyone you could think of who would stand out as the main suspect?"

"Well, there is the housekeeper, Daphne, I suppose," Craig said, "but she only found out that he was cheating on her that night. She wouldn't have had time to poison him, unless that was all an act. No, I'd be inclined to think it was Peaches. She has several nail salons, here and on the coast. She acts like a complete bimbo, but she's got the business know-how, you mark my words. Perhaps she found out he was cheating on her with Daphne and she did away with him."

"Peaches," Carl said thoughtfully.

"Yes, Peaches. I told the police I thought that, too."

"How did they respond?" I asked him.

"Do detectives ever respond to anything?" Craig asked me with a smile. "They merely thanked me for the information."

"And that's our cue to leave," Carl said, standing up. He reached out to shake Craig's hand. "Well, thank you for your information, too. Thanks so much, Craig, you've been ever so helpful."

I shook his hand as well. "Yes, I really appreciate it."

"Peaches," Carl said as soon as we were in the street, having attracted no more than a snooty glance from the receptionist as we left.

"Sorry?"

"Peaches," Carl repeated. "Do you really think she could be a suspect?"

"Never judge a book by its cover," I admonished him.

"Yes, but people always *do* judge books by their cover, Narel. You should know that."

I sighed. "Carl, let me guess what you're going to say next. We should go and visit Peaches now, right?"

Carl smiled. "Yes, but we can use the jewellery ruse this time. I'm sure Peaches would be most interested in the mention of an expensive piece of jewellery."

CHAPTER 13

Peaches' nail salon was only a few doors down from the advertising agency's office. There was a rather trendy café nestled between them, and I wondered if that was where Peaches and Stan had met. The big A-frame outside the door set out the prices on everything, nails, manicures, pedicures, as well as facials. It seemed this was more than a nail salon. "You know, I should have thought to book myself in to gather information."

"Me too," Carl said enthusiastically. "I usually only get work on my face when I go to Sydney, but it would be good to go to a local salon in between times. Do you think she does Botox?"

I looked at Carl. "Carl, you don't need Botox!"

"I already get Botox," Carl announced proudly. "Around my eyes."

I peered at his face. "Seriously?"

He nodded. "And I get fillers, too. Why do you think I look so good?" I had no answer for that. Carl brought the subject back to the matter at hand. "It's probably no use booking ourselves in for treatment just to get information, because Peaches herself mightn't do the treatment."

"But we could get information about her from the others," I pointed out.

Carl pounced on my idea enthusiastically. "Excellent idea, Narel!"

"But I won't book myself in today," I said. "I have to get back to the shop. I shouldn't leave it closed for too long."

Carl looked as though he was about to say something, but then thought better of it. "Okay, let's get to work."

This time, we were greeted with a far friendlier reception than the one at the advertising agency. "Hello, how can I help you?" a chirpy young woman asked.

"We just wanted to have a word with Peaches, if she's available," I said.

Peaches heard her name and came over. "Hi, were you at the party on Friday night?"

I nodded. "Could we speak to you privately?"

Peaches at once showed us into a tiny but spotlessly clean back room, with a small kitchen and eating area. The three of us sat on small but comfortable armchairs. "I just wanted to say how terribly sorry I am about Stan's passing," I said.

"Yes, we are so sorry," Carl said.

"You'll have to forgive my appearance," Peaches said sadly. "As you can see, I've been crying ever since."

I studied her face, but I couldn't see any sign of crying whatsoever. "That's perfectly understandable," I said, but Carl interrupted me.

"Oh my goodness, that's your crying face?" he said tactlessly. "You look absolutely fabulous, fabulous!"

I expected Peaches to be upset, but she beamed at Carl. "Thank you. How kind of you."

"Oh, it's the truth, honey. Do you do Botox? Fillers? I need to book in."

Peaches nodded, but before the conversation went in the wrong direction, I spoke. "I hope you don't mind us asking at such a time as this, but are you familiar with my chocolate shop, Coco Narel Designer Chocolates?"

She shook her head. "I don't eat chocolate," she said.

Of course you don't, I said silently. Aloud I said, "You've probably driven past my shop?"

"Yes, I have. Such a pretty shop."

"Thank you. I hope you don't mind us asking at such a time as this, but did you see the article on me in the local paper on Saturday morning?"

Peaches looked embarrassed, and nodded. "Yes, it's a pity you weren't wearing enough make up when that was taken. It completely washed you out."

"Err, yes," I said. I would have said more, but Carl spoke up.

"Narel didn't murder Stan," he said, "but the locals think she did. Mind you, the police know she didn't," he added hastily.

"I haven't had a single customer since that newspaper article came out," I said.

Peaches looked shocked. "Why, that's dreadful! I hope the locals don't start suspecting me."

"Just stay away from that nasty reporter," I said. "My problem is that I need to discover who killed Stan as soon as I can, or I'll go broke. I'm sure the police will solve it eventually, but I can't last that long without customers."

"No, of course not," Peaches said with obvious sympathy. "What a terrible predicament you're in."

I nodded. "Anyway, we were just speaking to Craig Cooper. In fact, we've come straight from his office. He didn't have any idea who could have possibly killed Stan, but he said you had a very good business brain and we should ask you."

Carl's eyebrows nearly shot off his face at my outrageous lie.

"It was that terrible lying housekeeper," Peaches said. "I'd bet my life on it. Did you see her that night, bursting in with her terrible lies that she and Stan were having an affair? As if he'd ever look at anyone like that!"

"Yes, it was a terrible scene, ruining his retirement party like that," I said, trying to inject sympathy into my voice. "Why do you think she did it?"

"I have no idea about the workings of that awful woman's mind. I asked Stan to fire her many times, but he wouldn't."

Carl and I exchanged glances. I was about to say something, when Peaches continued. "If I tell you something, can you keep it to yourselves and not let it go any further?"

We both hurried to assure her that we would not say a word.

"Stan told me that Daphne had a huge crush on him. He said he wanted to fire her, but she was blackmailing him."

"Did Stan say what she was blackmailing him over?"

Peaches very carefully dabbed a tissue under her eyes. "I know Stan wasn't any clean potato. I'm not a fool. I knew he was an aggressive businessman, but that was one of the things I admired about him. I knew some of his business dealings weren't quite above board, and it seems that Daphne found evidence of it. She'd been blackmailing him for some time."

"What sums of money were involved?" Carl asked her.

Peaches frowned, or at least she did the best imitation of frowning that anyone who'd had so much Botox could. "I don't think money was involved as such—she just wanted to stay on as his housekeeper. Because she had a huge crush on him, you see."

"Oh yes," I said, as if her words made perfect sense. "Can you think of anyone else who might have wanted to kill Stan?"

"Daphne did it," Peaches spat. "Mark my words, that awful Daphne did it."

On our way out, Carl booked in for fillers and Botox the following week. When we were safely out of earshot, Carl asked me, "Why didn't you go with the jewellery ruse?"

"It was going so well that I didn't have to," I said. "What do you think?"

"Yes, I agree. You did the right thing for sure. I thought that might be the reason. Now, this morning I researched Jake."

"What did you find out?"

"The only Jake I could find is a personal trainer at the gym. I mean, there could be plenty of Jakes in town, but he's the only one I've found so far. I've arranged it so we can spy on him tonight."

A horrible sinking feeling lodged itself in the pit of my stomach. "What do you mean, Carl?" I asked through clenched teeth. "What have you done?"

"I haven't done anything," Carl said innocently, "but we have to be at the gym at seven tonight."

"The gym?" I said in horror. "Out with it, Carl!"

Carl stopped, and shifted nervously from one foot to the other. "We're going to do a cardio class at the gym tonight at seven."

"Cardio? You're kidding, right?"

Carl continued to fidget. "I looked at the gym program, and it seemed to be the easiest. It said it was for beginners. I thought it couldn't be too bad, because there was a meditation and relaxation section at the end."

"How about we share it?"

"What do you mean?"

"What if you do the cardio part, and I do the meditation and relaxation section at the end?"

Carl laughed. "Oh Narel, you're too much."

"I'm not joking," I said. "You know I don't like exercise."

"Narel, you're always saying you want to get fit and healthy. You don't do any exercise, only an occasional walk. That's not good enough. Have you ever been inside a gym in your whole entire life?"

I had to admit that I hadn't.

"Good. Okay, then we can multitask. We can both get fit, and we can check out this Jake."

"What if he isn't the right Jake?" I asked him.

"I'm pretty sure he is," Carl said.

I sure hoped he was right. I didn't want to have to suffer through a cardio class for nothing.

CHAPTER 14

Five minutes into the class, I was certain going to die. Carl wasn't faring much better, but at least he didn't have to stop moving and catch his breath from time to time like I was doing.

"Grab a drink of water," the overly energetic Jake called out. "Now you've all finished your warm up, and we can get into the real fun stuff."

"That was just a warm up?" I managed to squeak, to nobody in particular. I waddled over to my drink bottle and reached for it. "Ouch!" My shoulder hurt. In fact, everything hurt. "Can we leave now, Carl?"

Carl's face was bright red. "No,…try…to… focus… Narel," he said very slowly and painfully. "The… relaxation… and… meditation… part… will… come… soon." He broke into a fit of coughing

"Not soon enough," I muttered.

I staggered back to my position and eyed Jake warily. He was bulked up, with huge shoulders and enormous musclebound legs. His manner was quite aggressive, but since I had never been in a gym before, I didn't know if that was usual or not.

"And now we'll have some more fun," Jake yelled at us. Clearly, Jake and I had very different ideas of fun. "Put some effort into it! You're not cheating me; you're only cheating yourselves! No pain, no gain!"

Jake then proceeded to lead us all in a series of movements that involved sliding at a rapid pace across the room while punching the air, and then sliding back across the room doing the same thing. Although it was supposed to be a class for beginners, the others seemed to have it all down pat. Carl and I were the only ones who didn't have a clue what we were doing.

At one point, I didn't quite get the choreography and was punched in the stomach by a woman coming the other way. I fell to the ground and just lay there, enjoying the rest, while the woman bent over me loudly voicing her apologies.

"Get up!" Jake yelled. "You, the skinny-fat woman!"

I struggled to my feet and found that my little rest had given me enough energy to speak. "Who are you calling fat?" I said to him.

"You're a fat person in a skinny person's body!" he yelled at me. "Come on now, put some effort into it! You need to get fit! Do you want to stay in that sorry state for the rest of your life?"

I shook my head, mainly because I had used all my available oxygen on my previous sentence. He was right—I did want to get fit, but I thought perhaps that a cardiac arrest might not be the right way to attain that goal. I wondered if there was a crash cart in the next room, because I sure as eggs thought I was going to need it.

I shot a look at Carl, but he avoided eye contact, probably because it would take too much energy for him. My breath was coming in ragged bursts and my throat burned. This was torture, pure and simple. Forget sleep deprivation; forget bamboo shoots under the fingernails. Cardio had to be the most effective form of torture in the world.

At first I was embarrassed to be performing so badly in front of everyone. Carl and I had chosen the spot at the back of the class, only that didn't help because Jake had everyone moving in all directions, and sometimes in circles around the room. That meant everybody could see my utter lack of ability. However, I soon stopped caring about how others saw me, and simply wanted to survive the session. It didn't help that Jake kept barking at me.

Just when I thought I was going to pass out, Jake announced that we had just finished our cool down. Now was the part I had been waiting for—the relaxation and meditation session. Jake yelled at us to lie on our mats. I didn't have to be told twice. I was the first one to lie flat out, followed soon after by Carl.

Jake yelled at us to relax and said he would put on relaxing music for five minutes. To my great relief, he then stopped talking, his loud, screeching voice replaced by the sound of soothing music.

I lay there, wondering why my toes hurt. I was sure even my toenails hurt. Muscles I didn't even know I had screamed in protest at the workout. All I wanted to do was get into a hot bubble bath. I wondered how many months it would take me to recover.

I didn't think I could meditate or relax, because my

muscles were cramping and sore. My legs and arms were burning, particularly my triceps. They were on fire.

There was a strange shift in the music, a strange sound like a loud pig grunting. At first, I figured it was some kind of bizarre experimental music. I wondered if Jake was still on the platform, but my eyelids hurt too much for me to open them.

The pig grunting noise grew louder and I heard some giggles. I opened my eyes. Carl was lying on the mat beside me, his mouth wide open, and omitting the most horrible snoring I had ever heard in my life.

"Time's up," Jake yelled, although not as loudly as usual. I figured he thought that was his soothing voice. "Remember, you're not cheating me, you're only cheating yourselves. I hope to see you all here next time. And you!" He pointed at Carl, who was blissfully unaware of his surroundings, as he was still snoring. "You! You're supposed to be relaxing and meditating, not sleeping!"

With that, he marched out of the room. Everyone else was on their feet, putting their mats away. I managed to roll over to my knees and crawl the short distance to Carl. I gently shook him awake. "It's over now, Carl. We can go."

"Over?" Carl said hopefully. "Are you sure?"

"The instructor's gone."

Carl groaned and he, too, rolled over onto his knees. We both tried to get to our feet, clutching each other for support, but it was very difficult to stand upright. Two kind and horribly fit looking ladies hurried over to help us. "I was like that the first time I came here," one of them said in what was an obvious lie. I mentally thanked her for her kindness.

"I don't think I'm cut out for this sort of thing," I said.

"Nonsense," the other lady said. "You did fine." She did, however, appear to be doing her best not to laugh.

"Everything hurts," Carl said. "I'm not sure I'm going to live."

The two ladies laughed uproariously at his remark, but it was clear to me that they were simply releasing their pent up laughter. We must have been a highly amusing spectacle throughout the whole class. "The instructor, Jake," I said. "Are all the other instructors like him?"

The first lady shook her head. "No, he's the hardest instructor by far."

"Well then, why do you do his class?" Carl asked in bewilderment.

"Because my husband only minds the kids at this time of night, and I can't get here at weekends."

"So Jake doesn't do weekends?" I asked them.

"No, he does the seven o'clock class and the eight-fifteen class on Friday nights."

The second lady interrupted her. "He works here Monday to Friday, but the only nights he works are Friday nights."

I nodded. "A friend of mine said she did a class last Friday night with a very hard instructor," I said. "Would that have been Jake?"

"Yes, I was here last Friday night doing that seven o'clock class," the second lady said. "I didn't see anyone new doing the class, though."

"Maybe she did the next class," I said. "Did Jake take them both?"

"I did the next class," the other lady said, "but I didn't see anyone new in that class, either."

"Did Jake take both classes?" I asked them. They both nodded. "Perhaps I got mixed up. Perhaps I don't have enough oxygen left to remember clearly," I added.

The ladies laughed and then said their goodbyes.

Carl clutched my arm. "Ouch, you're hurting me!" I said. "In fact, I think even the air is hurting me."

"I was just going to say that you did a very good job finding out about Jake," Carl said feebly. "Oh look, Narel. We have to go."

People were starting to file in for Jake's next class and were eyeing us strangely. Carl and I managed to get to the wall, but we both had trouble leaning down to grab our gym bags. My back couldn't quite bend that far. After we retrieved our bags, we walked out slowly, keeping one hand against the wall for support. When we were in the foyer, I went to sit down on the plush sofa, but Carl stopped me.

"No, Narel. You have to keep going. If you sit down, you won't be able to move again."

I thought that was good advice. The two of us managed to make it across the foyer while clutching each other. People looked at us strangely, but I was way past caring. Luckily, it wasn't far to Carl's car, but then neither of us could get in. "Narel, I'll crawl in first and move across your seat and then turn around and wedge myself into position, and then you crawl in," Carl said.

"That doesn't make any sense," I said weakly.

"What did you say?"

"I don't have the energy to repeat it," I said. "I think I need an energy drink, or maybe an IV glucose drip."

"I think I might have to stay at your place overnight until I recover," Carl said.

"Will Louis the Fourteenth be all right?" I asked him.

"Yes, there's plenty of water and food in his bowls."

"Sounds like a plan," I managed to say. Even speaking was an effort. It took us a full five minutes to climb into Carl's car. I was better off than Carl, because I was able to put the seat the whole way back and lie down, while Carl had to sit in a stooped position over his steering wheel. He let out cries of, "Ouch!" as well as other words that I am too polite to repeat, all the way back to my place.

Carl parked the car in my driveway and turned off the engine. We both looked at each other. "How do we get out?" he asked me.

"Maybe pretend Jake's in the back seat?" I said. That made us both laugh, but laughing hurt my abs so much that tears rolled down my face. "I'm in terrible pain," I managed to say when I could breathe again.

"Let's just get out of the car, no matter how much it hurts," Carl said. "On the count of five." I steeled myself. "One, two, three, four, five…"

I lifted my left leg out of the car and then lifted my right leg, and stood up carefully while hanging onto the car door. I waited until Carl came around to me, and then we both staggered to my front door.

Once inside, I collapsed on my sofa, and Carl dropped to my floor. "Oh, that feels good," he said. "Can you throw a few blankets over me, Narel? I won't be able to move until morning."

"Don't you want a hot bath?" I asked him.

"I would dearly love a hot bath, only I don't think I could make it to the bathroom quite yet. We need to hydrate."

"Good idea. I'll see how I feel in a few minutes, and I might be able to make us a hot chocolate."

"I was thinking more along the lines of water."

"Don't we need some sports drink? Jake did say we had to carb up. I have plenty of chocolates in the fridge. If we drink water and eat chocolates, wouldn't that be the same as a sports drink?"

Carl simply groaned.

"At least we know Jake isn't the murderer," I said. "He has an iron clad alibi. He couldn't put the poison in the fly agaric chocolates because he was at the gym the whole time."

I expected Carl to agree, but he was already fast asleep, evidenced by the horrible snoring sound coming from him, a sound so horrendous that it even drew Mongrel's attention.

Mongrel carefully walked out of his basket and pitter pattered over to Carl. He seemed intrigued by the sound. Mongrel bent over and looked at Carl's face.

At that inopportune time, Carl awoke. I figure the first thing he saw was Mongrel's face close to his own. He screamed, a bloodcurdling scream that made Mongrel run out of the room, his tail fluffed up like a toilet brush.

"Oh you scared him, the poor thing," I said.

Carl rolled over on his side and then managed to sit up. "All the oxygen has left your brain, Narel."

I lowered myself from the sofa, and got onto my hands and knees. "Quite possibly," I said. I crawled towards my kitchen, the thought of water and chocolates beckoning me. Carl crawled after me and somehow caught up with me. "You know, we're quite comical. I'd laugh, only it would kill my stomach muscles."

I had to agree. We both managed to fetch water and chocolates, but when we tried to sit at the table, our backs went into spasms. "Let's just stand here and eat the chocolates, and then we can go back and lie down in the living room," Carl said.

I agreed, but didn't have the strength to say it out loud.

After we had rehydrated, and carbed up on assorted chocolates, I was able to speak. "You know, Carl, I don't like Jake."

Carl snorted rudely, but then clutched his stomach. "Ouch, that hurts. No kidding! I don't like him either."

"I'm not just saying this because I don't like him—I think," I added. "I know Jake has an iron clad alibi, but what if he was in it with someone else?"

"But who?" Carl asked me.

I made to shrug, but my shoulder muscles locked up. "No idea," I said, and then broke into a coughing fit. It hurt my abs and every last one of my ribs. Who knew bones could ache?

"We should have asked more about him when we were at the gym," Carl said. "Only we were too oxygen deprived for our minds to work properly."

"Never mind, we can ask around town. I'm never going back to that gym again, Carl, and you can't make me."

Carl weakly held up one hand. "You'll get no argument from me."

"We suffered through that dreadful gym class and all we found out was that Jake had an alibi," I pointed out. "Hang on a minute, didn't you say he might be in it with someone else?"

Carl pouted. "I thought you said that, Narel. My memory hasn't been working since I started the class."

"Minnie! If Mick was right, and Minnie is seeing Jake, and it's the same Jake, then maybe the two of them were in it together."

I looked back up at Carl, but he had vanished. I struggled around to the other side of the table and saw him, fast asleep, on the floor.

CHAPTER 15

The following morning, I woke up on my sofa. There was no sign of Carl, so I figured he was still lying on the kitchen floor. I didn't think I could walk that far to check on him. I had thrown blankets over him the previous night and propped up his head on a pillow, and then I had crawled back to the sofa.

My abs hurt horribly, as did my arms and my legs. Even my ears hurt. In fact, there wasn't one part of me that didn't hurt—maybe my nose. I couldn't straighten up, so I walked, hunched over, to the bathroom where I ran a hot bath.

I poured a whole packet of Epsom Salts in the bath, as well as a little bubble bath, and then tentatively lowered myself in. It brought immediate relief, the hot water soothing away some of the aches in my screaming muscles.

I didn't know how I was going to get to the shop that day, but maybe there was no point. My time might be better served by trying to track down the murderer. Yes, that would be far more productive.

I had no idea of the time because my phone was in the other room, but I wasn't going to be any good to anyone unless I could walk upright. I lay in the bath until my fingers wrinkled, letting the water out at intervals and replacing it with hot water.

When I climbed out of the bath, I realised I had a little more movement in my muscles. That was when I remembered the liniment in my bathroom drawer. I reached for it and took off the lid, and made the mistake of smelling it.

"Whoa!" I exclaimed, as the smell of oil of wintergreen nearly knocked me on my back. Still, I slathered it all over me. It brought instant relief, so much so, that I was able to put on my bathrobe without too much trouble, and that was just as well, because as soon as I did, there was an insistent knocking on my front door.

I staggered to the front door, pleased that I was on the road to recovery. I opened the door to see Carl standing there, two polystyrene cups of coffee in his hands and a green shopping bag over his arm.

"Don't just stand there, let me in," he said. I stood aside, and he walked into the room.

"You're walking better than I am," I said with surprise. "I was just coming out to see if you were still on the kitchen floor."

"I left earlier this morning," Carl said. "I went home and then out to get supplies. Oh, you smell like I do. Did you cover yourself in liniment, too?"

I tried to nod, but it hurt too much, so I said, "Yes." I gingerly lowered myself to the sofa. Sitting didn't really help, and I winced when a sharp pain went through my right shoulder.

Carl handed me a cup of coffee, and then sat opposite me. "I have heat packs and cold packs in here. I don't know if we can use both at the same time. And I have these really cool Chinese herbal patches. They're adhesive, so we can just peel them off and stick them on ourselves. It's really helping me, that's why I'm walking better. I have some on my back." He stood up, turned around, and pulled up his shirt.

I gasped. Carl's back was entirely covered with adhesive patches. "It really works," he said. "I went to the Chinese herbalist and bought every one he had in stock." He threw a large packet to me. "Here, stick some on. You'll get instant relief, and if that doesn't work, we can try the cold and hot packs, but they're not self-adhesive."

My hand muscles were too sore for me to open the packet, so I grabbed a pen from the side table and stabbed it into the packet. That made a hole, and then I was easily able to undo it. I stuck one patch on the side of my neck. It smelt of oil of wintergreen too, or maybe I was just so covered in the stuff that I couldn't smell anything else. "Well, Carl, you were right! It's helping already." I took a few sips of coffee, and then stuck some herbal patches on my calves. I could feel them working.

"I ran into the mail lady when I was leaving the Chinese herbalist, and she told me that Stan Wellings' funeral is on today."

"I wonder how she found out? No one told us."

"That woman knows everything that happens in town," Carl said. "Anyway, we have to go."

"I know we have to go," I said slowly, "but do you think we will be well enough by then?"

Carl held up his box of Chinese herbal patches. "That's why I have these. Now go and get ready, Narel. It's already late."

I looked at my phone. "Crikey, is that the time? I haven't put a *Closed* notice on my shop door yet."

"We can do that on the way to the funeral," Carl said. "Just write, 'Closed, at a funeral,' and no one will be angry with you."

"I don't think anyone will turn up in the first place," I said. "I had pretty much decided not to open the shop today. I think my time would be more productively spent by finding out who killed Stan." Carl was acting a little funny, shifting in his chair, and I didn't think it was just from the pain of his muscles. "What is it, Carl?"

Carl pulled a face. "You won't like it, Narel."

"What is it?"

"That awful Graham Gibson put another article about you in the newspaper today."

"Show it to me. I know you have it."

Carl pulled a newspaper from his bag and threw it across the room to me. I caught it with two hands and looked at it. There I was, my photo taking up a sizeable portion of the front page. I was wearing a shocked expression in the photo. It was the photo taken at the rugby game, and the headline read, *Police Close in on Murder Suspect Narel Myers*.

"This upsets me, Carl," I said.

"I know, Narel," he said sadly. "I know."

I waved one finger at him slowly, because it hurt less

than shaking my head. "No, Carl. Don't you see what this means? It means that the police don't have a suspect."

"I see. You're thinking that if Graham Gibson knew the police had a suspect, then he would have done an article about the suspect rather than you."

"Yes."

"Maybe the police are keeping that from him."

"And maybe the police don't have a clue, just as we don't have a clue, either," I said to Carl.

"We've pretty much excluded The Purr-suader, and we've also put Craig Cooper and Peaches on the bottom of our list. We're not doing too badly, and the funeral will probably turn up more information. Hurry up and get changed, and then we'll have breakfast and go."

I picked up the bag of Chinese herbal patches and walked gingerly to my bedroom. I took off my bathrobe and put every available patch on me. I slapped them all over my back, and over my abs, on the side of my neck, on my triceps, my biceps, my deltoids, and on parts of which I didn't even know the names. I then slathered copious amounts of liniment on any skin that wasn't covered with a patch. I knew the patches on my neck were visible, but I really didn't care.

It hurt to put on my clothes. I had to sit on my bed and very carefully pull on my jeans. It seemed to take an age to get dressed. My knees had now kind of locked in position, and I felt like I was walking like a zombie or a robot.

Carl was in the kitchen making more coffee, and Mongrel was happily eating his breakfast. "You're such a good friend, Carl. I'd give you a hug, only it would hurt too much."

"You and me both," Carl said. "Why are you walking like that?"

"Perhaps I applied too many patches and too much liniment," I said. "I'm starting to get quite strange cold feelings in my legs."

"You'll walk it off," Carl said with confidence. "Let's have breakfast and then we'll head off to the funeral."

"What do we hope to find out at the funeral?" I asked him.

Carl held up his hands. "Who knows? But the police always go to the funeral of a murder victim on TV, so they must do that for a reason. They're busy people—they don't have time to go to funerals just to amuse themselves."

I didn't know how to respond to that, so I ate a banana.

"I'm impressed. You've eaten a banana before any chocolate."

"The banana is in front of me and the chocolates aren't, and everything hurts," I explained simply.

By the time we reached the funeral, I was walking a little better, but I was still in considerable pain. I was now quite used to the oil of wintergreen smell, so I was a little concerned when people sniffed the air and made comments in low tones about strange smells to each other.

I clutched Carl's arm. "Ouch!" He said, followed by, "What's wrong?"

"People are looking at me funny and whispering. They must recognise me from those terrible newspaper articles."

"Maybe it's just because you have all those herbal

patches stuck over your neck," Carl said. "Perhaps they think you're trying to give up smoking. They do look a bit like nicotine patches, after all."

"Is this your way of trying to make me feel better, Carl?"

He looked confused. We filed into the church, but to my dismay, Detective Clyde was standing right in front of us.

"Miss Myers, Mr Camden, fancy seeing you two here."

"Stan Wellings was eating my chocolates when he died, if you remember," I said, and then thought that was an incredibly silly thing to say.

"I like your new aftershave, Carl," Rieker said. I didn't know whether or not Rieker was being sarcastic, but Carl seemed to take it as a compliment.

He flashed Rieker a dazzling smile. "Thanks. It's Oil of Wintergreen."

"And you seem to be wearing the same aftershave, Miss Myers," Detective Clyde said snarkily.

"Carl and I had a difficult session at the gym last night," I said.

"Oh by the way, Detective Rieker," Carl said in a flirty tone, "I was at Peaches, the beauty therapist's, yesterday, and she told me that Daphne Delamare was blackmailing Stan Wellings. She said Stan and Daphne weren't really having an affair—but I think they probably were, who knows?—and she said that Daphne had uncovered evidence of Stan's unsavoury business dealings and was blackmailing him over it. Peaches seem to think Daphne didn't want money, but just wanted to stay on as his housekeeper, given that she had a crush on him."

"Thanks, Carl," Rieker said, and would have said more, only Clyde cleared his throat loudly and glared at Rieker.

I took Carl's arm. "Come on, let's sit in the back row so we can see everything." After we had taken our seats, I turned to Carl. "Maybe we should have brought cushions. These hard wooden seats are really hurting my butt."

"Me too," Carl said, "and that's the only place I haven't put some of those herbal patches."

"I don't think I'm going to be able to sit here for too long," I said, "and people are looking at me."

"Oh, it's just your imagination, Narel."

I wasn't so sure. "I feel really silly for telling Clyde that we went to the gym. He probably knows we went there to get information about Jake."

Carl shook his head ever so slightly. "No, he would have warned you to stay away if that had been the case. I don't think he's made the connection."

"Hence my problem," I said. "If only he *would* make the connection, and arrest somebody, and then my life could get back to normal. Oh gosh, Carl, it's that horrible reporter, Graham Gibson." I tried to slide down in my seat.

"He's gone to the front of the room," Carl said. "Maybe he won't see you."

"I can't take the risk," I said. "I've gotta go."

Carl clutched my arm. "You can't go, Narel."

"I'll just go to the bathroom and you can text me when he goes."

"But he'll stay for the whole service," Carl protested. "And we can't speak to anyone until after the service."

"Do you really think he'll stay after the service and chat to people?"

Carl shook his head. "No, he probably won't stay for the whole service. That would be too boring. You know, I bet he's just going to take some photos of whoever gives the eulogy, anything sensationalist he can find. Whatever you do, Narel, don't go near the coffin, because he'd like to take a photo of you there."

"You're pretty sure he won't stick around afterwards?"

"I don't think so."

"Carl, I'm going to the bathroom," I said again, more firmly this time. "Text me as soon as he goes, and I'll come back."

Carl pouted by way of response. The service was about to start, so I slid along to the end of the hard wooden pew and followed the signs to the bathroom. It was the only place where I would be safe from the reporter. He could hardly follow me in there. The bathroom was quite small and did not have anywhere to sit, so I didn't quite know what to do. I could hardly stand against the wall, looking aimlessly around, or pretend to apply make up for too long. People would wonder what I was doing in there.

I made up my mind. I would go into one of the toilet cubicles and read a book on my iPhone. At least that way, I wouldn't get bored.

It only took me a few minutes to get comfortable. It hurt my back to sit down, so I put one foot on the toilet seat and the other foot against the wall and leant back into a corner. It would have looked strange, had anyone happened to see me, but it felt quite good. I opened my phone app and selected a book I had only just started but was enjoying so far.

I shifted position after I read a few chapters. I

wondered why Carl hadn't texted me. I got out of the phone app and checked my messages, but there was nothing from Carl. I texted him to ask if the reporter was still there, and he at once texted back that he was.

"That pesky reporter," I said aloud, and then caught my breath. No matter, I was alone—I hadn't heard anyone else come in.

I read five more chapters before Carl finally texted me back. *Come back out here fast,* the text read. *Graham Gibson just left, and you'll never guess who's here!*

CHAPTER 16

"Who?" I asked Carl as soon as I slid along the hard wooden pew next to him.

He cast a surreptitious glance at the detectives, and then nodded to the front of the church. "Your worst nightmare."

I craned my neck, but all I could see was the back of people's heads. "Who?" I repeated.

"I couldn't see him because that pesky reporter was sitting directly behind him, but when he left, I saw who it was."

"Who?" I said again, this time through clenched teeth.

"Jake!"

I shuddered at the thought of his name, causing hot fire to stab at my abs, rendering me speechless.

"So he *is* connected with Stan in some way," Carl continued triumphantly. "I *knew* he was the murderer!"

I tapped Carl's arm, but he winced and rubbed the spot. "Ouch," he said plaintively.

"Just because we don't like the man, it doesn't mean he's the murderer," I pointed out. "Who's he sitting with?"

"Not Minnie, that's for sure."

I followed Carl's gaze, and Minnie was sitting on the other side of the room. "It's an older woman," I said.

Carl nodded. "Well, you've come at the very best part of this funeral." I raised my eyebrows, and he continued, "The end." His expression was heartfelt.

The minister was making an announcement, but I only heard the words, *cakes*, and, *coffee*. Carl leant across to me. "Don't get too excited—it'll be instant coffee."

Undaunted, I slid from the seat and followed the others out of the church, and down a small pathway into a community hall. I gave the detectives a wide berth. "I wonder who's paying for this funeral?" I asked Carl.

"I don't know, and that bothers me. There's a lot we don't know about Stan Wellings."

I had to agree. "What's our plan of action?"

"We need to find out who that woman with Jake is. Hang on a moment, do you think she's Daphne, the housekeeper?"

"I've only seen her from behind so far," I pointed out. "The only previous time I saw her, she was dressed in an apron, and she was screaming. This woman looks quite elegant and well-dressed from the back. I won't know until she turns around. She seems to be the right height, not that I was taking much notice of what Daphne looked like at the party, given that I didn't know a murder was about to take place."

"True, true. Let's skirt around here and get a look at her face."

Carl and I made our way to a long white trestle table

covered with what looked like white sheets in lieu of tablecloths. I eyed the cakes suspiciously. "I'm starving, but I don't think there's anything here that I can eat."

"Or drink, for that matter," Carl added. "Narel, quick, there's the woman."

I took a good look at the woman's face. "Yes, I'm pretty sure it's Daphne. What do you think?"

"I think so, too. Is she Jake's mother?"

I frowned. "Possibly. Or aunt? He's sticking close to her."

Just then, Peaches approached a young couple, skirting dangerously close to Daphne as she did so. Jake took Daphne's arm and moved her to one side. Daphne appeared to be resisting, so Jake escorted her out of the room.

"You stay here and watch what's going on," I whispered to Carl. "I'm going to follow them."

Jack and Daphne didn't go far—they both stopped just outside the community hall, right next to the wilted roses. "Mum, I'm here to support you, you know that," Jake said.

I smiled. So he was Daphne's son, after all. I wondered if the two of them were in it together. Perhaps Daphne did manage to poison the chocolates, although I didn't see how that was possible. And Jake had an alibi.

Jake was still talking. "I don't know why you're crying over that two-timing fool. I told you he was no good for you." Jake's remarks were punctuated by muffled cries from Daphne. "You should be glad he's dead!" Jake said in a raised voice. "You should save your sympathy for whoever killed him!"

When he didn't speak again, I hurried back to Carl, and repeated the conversation. "Well, if Daphne did somehow kill him, it obviously wasn't with Jake's help," Carl said sadly. "I so wanted to think Jake was the murderer."

"He *is* a murderer," I said. "A muscle murderer."

"Narel!"

I spun around to see Miriam Moreton standing there. Her eyes were red and puffy. "It was a lovely service," I said, hoping she hadn't noticed that I was absent throughout the entire event.

Miriam sniffled. "Yes, it was. I hope Peaches and Daphne don't cause another scene."

"I saw Jake take his mother outside just then," I said. "I think he's keeping an eye on her. By the way, did Minnie and Jake ever date?"

Miriam looked horrified. "No. I don't think they like each other at all. Jake wanted Daphne to quit and leave the Wellings. He's never had a good word to say for Stan, or Minnie, for that matter. A most unlikeable young man."

"That's for sure," Carl said with feeling.

"Have you found out who owns that piece of jewellery?" Miriam asked me.

For a moment, my mind went blank. It took me a moment to realise she had given me the guest list on the pretence of me searching for the owner of a piece of jewellery.

"No, not yet," I said, wondering how I could change the subject in a hurry. "Oh look, there's Minnie. Carl and I had better pay our respects."

I grabbed Carl's arm and dragged him away from Miriam. "Do you think she suspects anything?" I asked him.

Carl shook his head. "Of course not, Narel. You worry too much. You have to learn how to chill."

Minnie was standing by herself in a corner, looking ever so bored. "I'm so sorry about your father," I said to her.

She looked down her nose at me. "And you are?"

"Narel Myers, and this is my friend, Carl Camden. Miriam Moreton asked me to make the chocolates for your father's event."

She crossed her arms over her chest. "You have some nerve, coming to my father's funeral. I'm surprised the police haven't arrested you by now."

"Narel isn't a suspect," Carl snapped. "The police are looking for someone with an actual motive. Are you the sole heir?"

"I suggest the two of you leave before I call security," she said.

I was going to say something, but Carl took me by the arm and pointed me at the exit. "She's a real..." I began, but Carl interrupted me.

"Yes, she sure is. Let's leave in a hurry before we draw any attention to ourselves."

As we walked through the winding path leading from the community hall in the church to the parking area, I didn't see any sign of Jake or his mother. "Who's looking likely now?" I asked Carl.

"Your guess is as good as mine," Carl said. "From what you overheard, either Daphne didn't do it, or she did it without the knowledge of her son."

"If Daphne did it, then she had to be in it with someone else. Actually, that would explain why she created the diversion, so her accomplice could put the poison in the chocolates."

Carl shook his head, and pressed the remote to open his car. "But that brings us back to the key to the whole problem," he said. "By the night of his retirement party, Stan had already received a fatal dose. Whoever poisoned him had to know that."

"What makes you say that?" I said, gingerly lowering myself into Carl's car.

"Because nobody is going to poison someone with a poison that they know nothing about, are they? Unless they were pressed for time, of course. No, whoever poisoned Stan with death cap mushrooms knew whatever they needed to know about them. Sure, the second dose that night polished him off more quickly, but the question remains—why the second dose? If we can figure that out, then we will have the solution."

"I've thought about it until my head hurts," I said. "All I can think of is that the murderer wasn't at the party, and giving him a second dose at the party gave the murderer an alibi."

Carl started the car and slowly pulled out onto the road. "Which brings us back to the problem of who had access to the chocolates. Let's leave the Cat Whisperer aside for a moment. You made the chocolates, Narel, and then we took the chocolates to the party. Did we leave the chocolates alone at any time?"

I didn't have to think on that long. "No, we didn't, but we weren't staring at them the whole time. You know, it would have been easy for someone to put those poisonous tops on them."

"Are you thinking Miriam?"

I nodded. "She was the first one there, and she did go over to the chocolates and have a good, long look at them. She had the opportunity to put the poison caps on them. And don't you think it's strange that she ordered fly agaric mushrooms specifically? Why didn't I think of this before?"

"Everything's easy in hindsight," Carl said sagely. "How do we question her again?" Carl pulled up outside my shop, but kept the engine running.

"Aren't you coming in?"

He shook his head. "I need to get back and rearrange my whiteboards, and I'm a little behind on my work, too. I want to put Miriam at the top of the suspects list, and lower Minnie and Jake, maybe even take them off their own whiteboards."

"I've got it!" I exclaimed, sticking my head back in the car. "Why don't we take Miriam a nice box of handmade chocolates and spin her some story—perhaps say something like all the chocolates were confiscated by the police and we wanted to give her some to make up for it, or something like that."

"Yes, we'll play it by ear," Carl said.

I sighed at the typical response from Carl. "When should we do it? Should we go to her home, or take them to the office?"

Carl appeared to be thinking it over for some time. "If we go to her home, that will be twice we've turned up uninvited, so I think we should go to her office. How about we go just before five? She would be in a good mood, because she would be about to leave work for the day."

"Great idea. She'll also be in a hurry to tell us whatever

we want to know because she'll want to go home. That might make her a bit careless."

"You're an optimist, Narel."

I waved and shut the door. I turned around and walked straight into somebody. "Sorry," I said automatically, and then saw who it was. "Borage! Sorry, Tom."

Tom smiled at me, which made my knees go weak. *Get a grip, Narel,* I silently said to myself. *You're a grown woman.* Aloud, I said, "I was just at Stan Wellings' funeral. Would you like to come into my shop? I can make us some hot chocolate."

Tom said that would be lovely, and followed me into my shop. "Business hasn't picked up?"

"Dead as a doornail." I shook my head sadly. "And people were giving me strange looks at the funeral today. Not only that, Minnie Wellings was outright rude to me. She thinks I killed her father."

Tom's eyes filled with sympathy. "I know it's hard times at the moment, but try not to let it get to you too much. The police will arrest someone sooner or later, and then your shop will go back to normal."

"My concern is that the damage will be done by then," I said. "Anyway, enough sad talk. I'll make you a hot chocolate."

Soon Tom and I were sitting in my back room. A buzzer always alerted me when customers passed through the open door, although I was fairly sure the buzzer wouldn't go anytime soon. I offered Tom a tray of assorted chocolates. He ate several before speaking. "When do you think you'll start your search for a house?"

I was at once dismayed. Was this a business call? I must

have hesitated too long, because Tom spoke again. "You probably have too much on your plate to worry about things like that now. Anyway, we can discuss it over dinner. I came to tell you that I'll be out of town for the next few days, but would you let me take you out to dinner Friday week?"

I tried not to look too delighted. "Yes, that would be lovely. And getting a house is definitely next on my agenda. As soon as the police make an arrest, the first thing I'll be doing is looking for a house. I'll put my house on the market then too, because I'll need to get it ready for sale. I can't concentrate now, not with this hanging over me."

"You can instruct your lawyer to draw up a contract now," Tom said. "Sometimes they do it very quickly, depending on your lawyer, but sometimes it can take weeks. Are you familiar with the system in New South Wales?"

I shook my head.

"A real estate agent can't put your house on the market in New South Wales until he or she has a copy of the contract from the lawyer or the conveyancer," Tom said. "Then someone can make an offer, pending a pest and building inspection, maybe pending finance, too. They then exchange contracts after that, and settlement is usually thirty to forty days after that."

"I didn't realise it was such a long, drawn out process," I said.

"Yes, the Queensland system is much better," Tom said. "Someone simply writes their offer on a contract, and if that's countersigned, then their finance has to be approved within fourteen days and settlement is a further fourteen days after that. It's so much faster than New South Wales."

"I suppose it doesn't really matter all that much to me," I said. "I'll move into the new house as soon as I legally can, and if my house takes ages to sell, it won't be the end of the world. I hope Mongrel doesn't mind moving to a new house. The poor cat's had such upheaval in his life."

"I'm sure Mongrel will be happy to go wherever you are, Narel," Tom said with a smile.

My heart melted, and so did my chocolate. I looked down and realised I had been clutching a hazelnut chocolate tightly and now the chocolate was oozing through my fingers. "Oh gosh. I hadn't realised I was so tense. It's those terrible newspaper articles," I said, jumping up to wash my hands at the little sink behind me.

"Yoo-hoo!" came Carl's dulcet tones from my front door, just as the buzzer went off. I heard his footsteps striding across my polished wooden floor. He stuck his head around the door. "Oh, my goodness! I had no idea you had company, Narel, or I wouldn't have butted in. You shouldn't have left the front door open. Thank goodness you're both not in a state of undress!"

CHAPTER 17

My cheeks burned. "Carl!"

Carl waved one hand at me. "Come on, Narel. We're on the move. Suspect alert!"

"Whatever are you talking about, Carl?" I said crossly, putting my hands on my hips.

"I just spotted Miriam Moreton taking a seat at that café right next to the agency, and she was alone," Carl said. "Grab some chocolates and let's go there. We can cross examine her under the guise of being friendly."

I cast a rueful look back at Tom. I hoped he was as disappointed as I was. After I said goodbye to Tom and locked the door, I followed Carl down the street in the direction of the café. "Great timing, Carl."

Carl laughed. "It's not as if you're never going to see him again."

I had to admit that he had a point.

When I reached the café, I saw that Miriam, indeed, was alone and was sitting at the back of the café. "She probably just wants to be by herself," I told Carl. "After all, she has just been to her boss's funeral."

Carl ignored me and walked straight over to Miriam. "May we join you?" He sat opposite her without waiting for her to respond.

"Only for a minute," I said. "We were on our way to your office to give you these chocolates when we saw you in here. We're sorry to intrude." I handed Miriam the box of chocolates. "They're handmade," I added. "I felt so bad about the other night, with the police confiscating all those chocolates, so I selected some just for you."

Miriam smiled wanly. "That's a lovely thought. Thank you."

A waitress appeared and hovered over us. "Would you like drinks before you order?"

Carl shook his head. "Nothing for us, thanks. We're only here for a minute."

The waitress frowned and then disappeared. Carl turned his attention to Miriam. "Will you be out of a job now?" he asked her, as tactless as ever.

I stood on his foot. "Ouch!" he said.

Miriam shot him a strange look. "No, Craig is taking over Stan's position, so I'll now be Craig's personal secretary."

I wondered if I should revisit Craig as a suspect. "Will you enjoy that?" I prompted her.

"Oh yes, I should imagine it will be quite a relief."

"Why you say that?" Carl asked her.

Miriam's cheeks flushed, and she fidgeted with her coffee.

"State secrets?" Carl asked her with a laugh.

His remark seemed to relax Miriam. "Oh well, if you must know, it was quite stressful working for Stan."

"Wasn't he nice to you?" I asked her.

"Yes, he was very nice to me," she said. "He gave me lots of little bonuses. It did put me in an awkward position, though."

I frowned. "What do you mean?"

"Shall we say that if someone is a personal secretary to a man who is seeing more than one woman, it usually falls to the secretary to keep the women apart. I had to cover for him on more than one occasion."

The penny dropped. "Aha, so you knew about both Peaches and Daphne?" I asked her.

Miriam nodded. "Yes, I had to make sure they didn't find out about each other."

Carl leant forward. "Who do you think told Daphne about Peaches that night?"

"No idea." Miriam twirled her latte glass around a few times. "Their timing was bad, though."

"All the timing was very good," I said.

Miriam looked up at me. "What do you mean?"

"Someone poisoned those chocolates, the fly agaric chocolates you asked me to make. Daphne caused a diversion so the murderer could have put the poison in the chocolates at that point."

Miriam appeared to be thinking it over. "And Mick caused a scene, as well."

I agreed. "So there were two big scenes, and both would have given someone the opportunity to put poison in the fly agaric chocolates, because everyone was looking at the big argument."

"We wanted to ask Minnie if she invited Mick, but I think she thinks I killed Stan," I said.

"But that's ridiculous!" Miriam said.

I raised my eyebrows at her vehemence.

Miriam looked somewhat abashed. "She's a spoilt little good-for-nothing, that one. While I didn't approve of Stan's methods, either in his personal life or in his business life for that matter, he certainly didn't deserve a daughter like that. She hasn't done an ounce of work in her life, that one. She was always very rude to me."

"Did she ever date Jake, Daphne's son?" I asked her.

"Jake?" Miriam looked puzzled. "Not as far as I know. She did spend some time with Mick, and that made Stan very angry. He never mentioned her dating anyone called Jake. I'm sure he would have told me if Minnie was dating Daphne's son."

Carl groaned and put his head in his hands. He rested his elbows on the table.

I decided to come right out and ask her. "Who do you think murdered Stan?"

Miriam finished the rest of her coffee before answering. "That question has kept me awake at night. The police took me down to the station and gave me the third degree, but that was on Saturday, and I haven't heard from them since, thank goodness. It was the fly agaric chocolates, you see."

"What do you mean?" Carl asked her.

"He was poisoned with death cap mushrooms, and I had requested that you make fly agaric mushrooms. The police thought that was altogether way too much of a coincidence, so they thought I killed him." Her voice broke and she took a moment to compose herself before pushing on.

"Who else knew you asked me to make fly agaric mushrooms?" I asked her.

"You sound like the police," she said with a smile. "I'm quite sure I didn't actually tell anyone, although there were the emails between us."

"Were those emails only on your work computer?" I asked her.

She nodded. "Yes. I see what you mean; anyone could have looked at my computer when I wasn't there."

"And everyone knew you were organising the retirement party for Stan, didn't they?" Carl said.

"That's right, and I'd been organising it for weeks. All the information about it was on my computer, and as my desk is in the small reception room outside Stan's office, anyone had access to it. Of course, no one was supposed to touch my stuff, but anyone would have been able to do so easily, if they really wanted to."

"So it seems that someone saw that you had asked me to make fly agaric mushrooms as a special present for Stan, and thought they would add some poison mushrooms to them."

"What a devious mind the murderer must have," Carl said. "It doesn't sound like the work of an ordinary run-of-the-mill murderer."

"Is there such a thing as an ordinary murderer?" I asked Carl, but he simply shrugged.

"Can you smell that strange smell?" Miriam asked me. "If I don't know how to describe it, but it's sort of like pine needles, only very strong."

"Oil of wintergreen," I said automatically. "Sorry about that. Carl and I are covered in liniment."

"Yes, we did a cardio class last night." Carl rolled his eyes. "It was nearly the death of us both." He realised what he had said and his hand flew to his mouth. "Oh, I'm so sorry. You must miss Stan."

Miriam's face fell. "It's such a shock, and it's even more of a shock that he was murdered. I know this sounds a strange thing to say, but it would have been easier to take if he had just died of a heart attack, you know what I mean?"

I nodded. "Yes, that makes perfect sense."

"Do you think Craig Cooper did it?" Carl asked Miriam.

I was about to admonish Carl for being so forthright, but Miriam laughed. "Goodness me, no. If he was going to murder Stan, he would have murdered him years ago."

Something had been niggling at the back of my mind, and I just now remembered what it was. As Stan's personal secretary, Miriam was involved in his personal life as well as his business life. "Miriam, who's going to inherit Stan's estate?"

"Minnie. A shame he didn't leave it all to charity."

"So she's the sole heir?"

"I'm afraid so, the ungrateful little wretch."

Carl spoke up. "Are you absolutely positive?"

Miriam's eyes opened wide. "Do you think she did it?"

"I have absolutely no idea who did it," I answered honestly. "I suppose the obvious thing is to look at who stands to gain from the victim's death, and in this case, it seems to be Minnie."

Miriam shook her head. "But that would be like killing the goose that laid the golden egg," she said. "That girl wanted for nothing—he gave her whatever she wanted. There was no reason for her to kill him."

"Is that just a figure of speech, or did he actually give her everything she wanted? I mean *everything*?" I asked her.

"I see what you mean." Miriam nodded slowly. "He did refuse to buy her that Ferrari."

Carl made a strangling sound. "You're kidding! A Ferrari!"

"Yes, now you're getting the picture of what sort of girl she really is. Now I come to think about it, he actually didn't give her everything she wanted, not from her perspective, if you see what I mean."

I caught Carl's eye, and we stood up. "Enjoy your chocolates," I said to Miriam.

When we were back in my shop, I turned to Carl. "What did you make of that?"

He sighed long and hard. "I don't know, Narel. I thought it was Craig, but after we spoke to him, I thought he was innocent. I thought it was Peaches, but after we spoke to her, I thought she was innocent. And the same goes for Miriam. I suspected her, but after speaking to her, I don't really think she did it. I don't think I'm cut out for this detective work," Carl said sadly.

I patted him on the shoulder. "Let's look at what we do know. We know there were two big public scenes, and that they were probably distractions so someone could slip poison into the chocolate. And don't ask me why there were two distractions, because I don't have a clue. You keep saying if we knew why someone poisoned Stan for the second time, then that would lead us to the identity of the murderer."

Carl nodded. "I've been giving it a lot of thought, and I think the murderer did it to throw suspicion onto someone else."

"Like Mick? Or Daphne?"

"Actually, what you have just said is making me think."

"Think what?" I asked him, hoping he wouldn't draw out the answer like he usually did.

"I'm wondering if the murderer wanted to frame Mick, because Mick was actually at the party for some time and had access to the chocolates."

"Good thinking!" I said. "And everyone saw Daphne come in, yell at Stan, and then leave, and she didn't go anywhere near the chocolates, whereas Mick was there a lot longer before Stan saw him."

Carl scratched his chin. "If only I had my whiteboards here. Okay, if, and it's a big *if*, someone wanted to frame someone, then they were trying to frame Mick, and not Daphne."

"That makes perfect sense. But why have Daphne come in at all? Why the need for the second distraction? Whoever did it would have known that Stan would make a scene as soon as he saw Mick." I thought it over some more. "I think I've got it. What if Daphne was the distraction, and Mick was invited solely to be a suspect in Stan's murder? What if they were trying to frame Mick? That way, any scene would have been incidental, as they wouldn't have known in advance just how Stan would react to him. On the other hand, whoever told Daphne would have known she would create a huge scene. I think we have narrowed it down, Carl. We have to find out who told Daphne that Stan was dating Peaches."

CHAPTER 18

"I don't know how you talked me into this, Carl," I said, as Carl's car sped out of town. We were on our way to Stan Wellings' house.

"We need to question Daphne as soon as possible," Carl said. "It was your idea, Narel. Weren't you listening to yourself?"

"I didn't mean we had to speak to her right now," I pointed out.

"We have far too many suspects, so we need to narrow them down. Anyway, time is of the essence, because I've invited The Purr-suader to your place for dinner, Narel."

I groaned. "This day is just getting worse, Carl. The only thing that's been keeping me going all day is the thought of having a lovely long, hot bath, putting more herbal patches and liniment all over me, and then falling asleep on the sofa while watching The Voice."

"But I'll cook dinner," Carl said. "You know that."

"Yes, that's good of you to cook dinner when you invite someone over to my place without asking me first,"

I said dryly, "but it's just the thought of having to entertain someone when I'm so tired and when everything hurts."

Car laughed. "We won't be entertaining him, Narel. We'll be questioning him."

"But I thought we didn't suspect him any longer?"

"There's something that still niggles at me," Carl said seriously. "We haven't found out why he's in town. He is very well known, and this is a small country town. Why would anyone in their right mind come to this town?"

"You have a good point there."

"Yes, I know," Carl said. "So I'm planning to ask him exactly what he's doing in town. While I don't actually suspect him, I need to know the answer to that question to discount him as a suspect once and for all. You have to admit, it's fairly suspicious that he just happens to be in town right when Stan is murdered, and Stan stole his wife from him."

"We've already discussed that," I pointed out. "Surely he would have killed Stan years ago."

Carl ignored me, and pressed on. "And he did have access to the chocolates."

"But Mongrel likes him," I said.

Carl nodded. "Yes, and as we know, Mongrel is a very good judge of character. That's the only reason why The Purr-suader isn't at the top of my suspects list, because everything else fits. Do you think Mongrel is just luring him into a false sense of security?"

I looked over at Carl. "Are you out of your mind?" I said incredulously.

"Quite possibly."

"Kangaroo!" I yelled.

Carl slammed on the brakes, and a large grey kangaroo hopped in front of us. "Slow down, because that roo's friends might be right behind it," I cautioned him.

Carl did as I asked.

"Well, I suppose it's a good idea to find out why The Purr-suader is in town, because then we can truly exclude him as a suspect," I conceded. "I only hope he goes home early, because if he doesn't, I'm going to fall asleep right in front of him."

"I sure hope he isn't allergic to the smell of oil of wintergreen," Carl said. He drove out of the cover of trees, and we both gasped.

"I didn't even know this house was here," I said to Carl.

He shook his head. "Me either."

In front of us was a grand two storey Edwardian mansion. I knew there were grand homesteads just out of town; I had just never encountered one before. This was nothing short of magnificent. The red brick of the impressive building contrasted with the delicate white iron lacework. A five-storey central tower dominated the façade and overlooked the circular entrance driveway. It was just like something out of a movie.

"Wow!"

"I agree," I said. "Wow! They say the two main motives for murder are love and money. There sure is a lot of money involved here."

"I'll say!" Carl edged the car forward slowly. "I wonder where Daphne's house is?"

"I don't want to run into Minnie again," I said with dread.

Carl cut to the left of the mansion and followed a dirt track which wound its way beside a small creek. "There."

In front of us was a small Victorian cottage. It was cute, pale grey and charming. Climbing roses trailed along the wire fence, and wisteria climbed all over the gum trees that framed the cottage. "Someone lives there," Carl said.

"It must be Daphne's house. You know, Carl, I'm more anxious about this visit than the others. I don't have a good feeling about it."

"But she can't be the murderer; you said so yourself," he pointed out. "At no time did she have access to the fly agaric chocolates."

"You're right. It's probably just all the oil of winter-green fumes getting to me. I hope she doesn't order us off the place."

I approached Daphne's front door with trepidation. While Carl was always happy to play it by ear, I liked to have a solid plan. Carl knocked on the door, and Daphne opened it at once.

"Yes?" she said.

I sized her up. She wasn't overtly aggressive, but she had a manner about her that suggested she would brook no nonsense. I handed her the box of chocolates and she took them, probably by reflex.

"What are these?" she asked.

"I'm Narel Myers and this is Carl Camden," I said. "We're friends of Miriam Moreton's." This time I didn't feel guilty for the exaggeration. I don't know whether or not that was a good thing. "Miriam asked me to provide all the handmade chocolates for Stan's retirement party, and the police confiscated them all. I felt so bad about it that I'm taking everyone some of my best handmade chocolates and delivering them in person."

I wondered if that was believable—I don't think I would have believed it.

"I wasn't invited to the party," she said after a slight hesitation.

"Miriam said that you should have been," I lied again. "She was quite distressed that you weren't."

I looked at Carl, and he nodded furiously.

Until now, Daphne had been looking at us through the fly screen. She pushed it open. "Come in. Would you like a cup of tea?"

"Yes, please," Carl and I said in unison. In the country, it was a grave insult to refuse someone's offer of a cup of tea, whether you wanted one or not.

Daphne's house was small and cluttered, although spotless. She busied herself spooning tea leaves into a large pot, poured in the boiling water, and then put a tea cosy over the top.

"That's an absolutely gorgeous Edwardian mansion," I said to Daphne in an attempt to make conversation.

Her eyes lit up. "Yes, it is. Stan and Minnie only live in one part of it, though. It's too much work to keep it all running."

I noticed that she spoke of Stan in the present tense, and was grateful that she hadn't realised it. That probably would have upset her too much. "Do they run tours?" I asked her.

She shook her head, and then rattled around in a cupboard, soon producing a packet of biscuits. "Stan was thinking of it, but Minnie said she didn't want people going through her things. Of course, I did tell him that he could section off the private living quarters. I grew up in England, and that's the way things are done there. You don't have tourists nosing around someone's private living quarters."

She continued talking about her childhood in England, but I was only barely listening. I did notice that she showed absolutely no animosity towards Minnie. To the contrary, she spoke of her fondly. When she paused to take a breath, I spoke. "I truly am sorry about what happened to Stan, and I hope Minnie is managing okay."

Daphne shook her head. "That poor girl. She has no relatives left alive now, not with her poor father gone." She wiped her hands on her apron.

"But she has the big mansion," Carl said.

I glared at him.

"She'll sell it now," Daphne said, after shooting Carl a hard look. "It's too much work for just one girl."

Carl continued on in his tactless way. "Will she sell your house, too?"

Daphne did not seem concerned. "Yes, of course. It's all on the same property. There is this house, and then some old shearers' quarters out the back that have been renovated, and then a whole lot of other outbuildings as well. It will all go together. I'll give the poor girl a bit more time to grieve, and then I'll suggest she gets a good stock and station agent to do a clearing sale before the place goes on the market."

"Wise advice," I said in a monotone.

I was mentally moving Minnie to the top of Carl's whiteboard. She had the opportunity, and she certainly had the motive. Her father's death would leave her a millionaire several times over. She could certainly buy more than one Ferrari. Yet if she was the murderer, why create the two distractions at the party?

I needed to ask Daphne who told her that Stan was having an affair. I didn't want to make her angry, and it looked as though she was the type of person to get angry quite easily. In fact, I had seen an example of her anger only the other night. Of course, those were extreme circumstances, but I didn't want to provoke her.

"Please don't think I'm speaking out of turn," I began carefully, "but I'm awfully sorry about the whole thing with Peaches. There is nothing worse than a cheating man. Who told you about Stan and Peaches?"

I held my breath and carefully watched her reaction. Finally, she spoke. "It was my son, Jake. He never liked Stan. He always said, 'Get rid of that loser—he'll never marry you.' In fact, Jake constantly nagged me about it, so much so that I was even relieved when weekends came about, because Jake always worked at the gym all weekend." I tried to think of something to say, but she continued. "But it turned out that Jake was right, after all. Stan was always promising that he would marry me, but he never publicly acknowledged me as his girlfriend."

"Didn't you think that was strange?" Carl asked her.

"Things are always obvious in hindsight," I hastened to add.

Daphne nodded slowly. "I should have listened to Jake. I did think it was strange that Stan never brought anyone from work home, only Miriam on occasion for dinner, but when I asked him about it, he said he liked to keep his work and personal life separate."

"But how did he plan to keep you and Peaches apart, given that he was retiring?" Carl asked, again tactlessly.

Daphne frowned. "I hadn't thought of that. I have no idea, to tell you the truth. I've just had one shock after the other lately, first finding out that Stan was two-timing me, and then he was murdered."

"Well, hopefully the police will arrest the murderer soon and put your mind at rest, at least on that score," I said.

"The police!" she spat angrily. "Fat lot of use they are! They've questioned me every day. They even made me go down to the station, and they treated me like a common criminal."

"Why, that's ridiculous," Carl said. "You couldn't possibly have done it."

"Tell that to the police!" Daphne said in a raised voice.

Just then the fly screen banged and Jake stormed into the room. "Why are you upsetting my mother?" he yelled at us.

"They're not upsetting me," Daphne said. "The police were the ones who upset me. Why are you always causing trouble, Jake? You always go off like a bull at a gate without thinking first."

Jake's face went bright red. "The police? What do the police have to do with it?" He grabbed a knife out of the nearby butcher block and brandished it at us. "Get out of here!" he bellowed.

Carl and I didn't need to be told twice. We jumped from our seats and ran to the front door, Daphne calling out apologies after us.

Carl's wheels spun in the gravel, and he took off down the driveway at a far greater speed than he had driven in. "It's him; it's him," he said over and over again while tapping the steering wheel with one hand.

"But he had an alibi," I said. "He must be in it with someone else."

"Who?" Carl said. "Minnie?"

I took long slow breaths to calm my nerves. The scene with Jake had been terrifying. "Miriam didn't think that Jake and Minnie were seeing each other," I said. "Who told us that they were dating? Mick, wasn't it? Do you think Mick and Jake are in it together?"

Carl shook his head. "No, that doesn't make sense. If Mick and Jake are in it together, then Mick wouldn't have told us that Minnie and Jake were seeing each other."

"This whole thing has just put me in a head spin," I lamented. "None of it makes any sense. Do you think Jake and The Purr-suader are in it together?"

Carl shot me a look. "You know, Narel, that might not be as crazy as it sounds."

CHAPTER 19

Carl turned into a side road.

"What are you doing?" I asked him.

"We're going to follow Jake. I'm sure he's the murderer, Narel. I'd bet anything that he's in it with someone who was at the party that night."

"So you think two people were involved in murdering Stan?"

Carl nodded. "Yes, I do." He slowed down and then turned the car back the other way. "He won't see us from here if he drives straight past."

A curious black and white cow came and stared over the fence at us. Carl leant out the window. "Shoo!" he said. "You'll give the game away!"

I had to laugh. "Carl, Jake won't notice a cow staring at something. Cows always stare at something."

"Cows are welcome to stare at whatever they want, so long as it's not me," Carl said with a pout. "I hope this dust settles down, because it's a dead giveaway that someone has driven down this road."

"Even if Jake sees the dust, he won't think it's us hiding under a tree, with a cow staring at us, waiting to follow him to his accomplice," I said. "And back to the subject—if Jake *was* involved, it only stands to reason that the other person was at the party that night, because Jake had an alibi. Daphne said Jake told her that Stan was having an affair, and that also fits. Daphne went to the party and created a scene, giving whoever Jake's accomplice was the chance to poison the chocolates."

"The one thing that bothers me," Carl said, "is why Mick was at the party."

"We can rule out a genuine invitation, because Minnie hadn't been involved with Mick for a while. That means it was either Minnie, or someone who had access to her phone. Or perhaps someone was setting up Mick to take the fall."

"You know," Carl began, "all this thinking can't be good for us. It's making my head spin. How about we just follow Jake, and then everything will fall into place."

"I hate to disappoint you, Carl, but what if Jake just goes back to the gym? Exactly how long do you intend to follow him for? You invited The Purr-suader to my place for dinner tonight, remember?"

"I didn't say it was going to be easy, Narel," Carl admonished me. "The journey of a thousand miles begins with one step."

I held my hand. "Please never say that again." I reached into my purse for another Chinese herbal patch. I peeled off the protective layer and stuck one on the side of my neck. "Would you like one, Carl?"

"Would I ever," he said with feeling. "Can you spare five?"

We sat there for some time, peeling the protective layers off herbal patches and sticking the patches all over us. "You know, I just remembered something. Remember that Daphne said Jake worked weekends?"

"Yes!" Carl exclaimed. "I did notice that. I made a mental note to tell you afterwards, but being chased out of the house with a knife made me forget everything."

I pulled a face. "You and me both. That means Jake does something on weekends that his mother doesn't know about."

"You know, Jake might simply be some sort of common criminal and not the murderer, after all. I hope he hurries up, because the forecast is for heavy rain."

I was about to reply, when Carl grabbed my arm. "It's Jake's car!"

"Lucky we saw it when we ran out of Daphne's house," I said.

"It's probably the only car around for miles that isn't a ute," Carl said. "I'm excited, Narel. He might lead us straight to his accomplice."

"Or he might lead us straight to the gym," I said.

To my relief, Jake wasn't driving over the speed limit. Speed still terrified me, and even though I was getting better at being a passenger, I was still a long way from buying my own car. Still, I was making improvement and that was the main thing.

I was zoning out, looking at the scenery of paddock after paddock dotted with sheep and the occasional cow, when Carl tapped my arm. "That's not the way to the gym!" he said with excitement.

"It's probably just the way to McDonald's or KFC."

Carl snorted rudely. "Jake certainly wouldn't go near any fast food places."

"I didn't mean it literally," I pointed out. "I just meant that he could be going anywhere. Maybe he's going to do his grocery shopping. Maybe he's going to see his steroid supplier. Who knows?"

Just then the rain came down in buckets. Carl switched on his lights and put the wipers onto maximum. "I can't see a thing," Carl said, leaning over the steering wheel. "I'm going to have to speed up and sit just behind Jake. He won't know it's me in the rain, and I need lights to follow, otherwise I won't be able to see where we're going."

The car in front slowed down, no doubt due to the heavy rain, and made its way through some of the side streets on the outskirts of town. "I don't like this," Carl said.

I sat upright. "What's wrong?"

"This road goes down past the golf course. It's a dead end road. What if he sees us?"

"It's raining too hard to see anything," I said. "Don't worry about it. You can turn around now and go back if you want. Maybe he's just going to play golf."

"In this rain?" Carl said.

We had come to the end of the road and Carl turned the car slowly. "Can you see anything? The rain's easing now. Where did he go?"

"No idea." I rolled down my window to peer out. I stuck my head out the window, and just to my left was Jake's car. Jake was walking up the steps of a little cottage, and standing in the doorway was Minnie. Jake turned around and looked straight at me.

I hit the button to roll up the window and leant back. "Quick, Carl, drive!"

"What happened?"

"Quick! Drive off!" It wasn't until Carl sped up that I breathed a sigh of relief. "I saw Minnie at the door of the cottage back there, and Jake was walking up to her. It must be their little love nest."

"Did he see you?"

"I think so. Then again, I can't be sure. I thought he was looking straight at me. Carl, what are we going to do?"

"We'll go to your place, and I'll make dinner," Carl said calmly. "Before I start dinner, I'll call Detective Rieker and tell him what you saw."

"I can't believe that Minnie would kill her father," I said in disbelief. "Minnie and Jake, in it together."

Carl turned onto the main road. "We don't know that for sure. At least if I tell Rieker that we saw the two of them together, and how Jake acted at his mother's house, Rieker should be able to connect the dots."

"It all fits now," I said, thinking it over. "Mick said Minnie texted him, and at first we thought someone had gained access to her phone. Now it seems she probably did text him. She wanted suspicion to be thrown onto him. So Minnie and Jake didn't intend there to be two diversions, after all. They wanted Mick to get the blame for killing Stan, and Jake told his mother about Stan's involvement with Peaches so she could create the diversion. That must have been when Minnie poisoned the chocolates."

Carl stopped his car in my driveway. "Oh good, The Purr-suader isn't here yet. Yes, I do think you're right,

Narel. As you say, it all fits. Still, that doesn't mean there isn't another explanation. Maybe three or more people are in it together. Stan must've been worth millions, and if his fortune is divided a few ways, everyone would still get enough."

I shuddered. "Please tell me you don't think The Purr-suader was in it with them?"

"It remains a possibility," Carl said solemnly. "I'm going to ask him what he's doing in town. Anyway, let's get inside. I'll call Rieker and tell him what's going on."

"And make sure you tell him that you invited Peter The Purr-suader for dinner," I said. "Maybe the detectives know something about him that we don't. It will put my mind at rest if they know he's at my place."

"Please don't worry about it too much," Carl said. "Don't forget, Mongrel likes him."

I bit my lip. "What if he hypnotised Mongrel or something?"

Carl clutched his stomach. "Oh Narel, you crack me up. Please don't make me laugh until my muscles recover."

Carl and I made a run for the door, but the rain was now only light. I hurried to feed Mongrel, while Carl made the call to Rieker. I went to my bedroom and changed, putting on some dry clothes. I rubbed some liniment into my back, arms, legs, shoulders, neck, and feet. "There, that should about do it," I said to my reflection in the mirror.

When I walked out, Carl was already in the kitchen making a start on dinner. "What did Rieker say?"

Carl turned around. "It went straight to voicemail. I left him a message, and I texted him as well."

I frowned. I was a bit worried about The Purr-suader

coming for dinner. I was worried that Rieker didn't know about it, but there was nothing we could do about that now. I was sure Rieker would come across Carl's message sooner or later. And then there was the fact that Mongrel did seem to like The Purr-suader.

I jumped at the knock on the door. "He's here already," I said. "Hasn't he ever heard about being fashionably late?"

Carl caught my arm. "Look out the window first, and make sure it's him and not Jake."

"You don't think Jake would come after us?" I said in horror.

Carl shook his head. "No, but it's better to be safe than sorry."

I looked out the window, but couldn't see a car. My pulse increased and I broke into a cold sweat. "There's no car out there. It might be Jake."

I crossed to the front door and called out, "Who is it?"

"It's me, Peter Patterson, the Cat Expert, The Purr-suader."

I peeked around the door, and it was indeed Peter. "Come in," I said urgently. "I couldn't see your car outside."

"I got a taxi," Peter explained. "I thought maybe there would be wine with dinner, and I didn't want to drink and drive."

I locked the door behind him. "Please come in. I'm afraid dinner might be a while. Carl and I got held up this afternoon. We're running late."

Peter sat on the sofa, and placed his cat training bag next to him. Carl sailed into the room and pressed a glass of bubbly into his hands. "Cheese platter coming up!" Carl said before exiting.

I sat opposite Peter, and then thought I should maybe get myself a glass of bubbly, but before I could leave my seat, Carl reappeared and handed me one. "Thanks, Carl. Would you like any help with dinner?"

Carl declined. I expected he wanted what he called a proper dinner, and that was a dinner without chocolate, or to be precise, the main course without chocolate. It wasn't to my personal taste, far from it, but I was trying to get healthier.

Carl presently returned to the room with a huge cheese platter. Peter helped himself. Carl came straight to the point. "So, Peter, how are you enjoying life in this little town?" Before Peter could answer, Carl pressed on. "Do you happen to know somebody by the name of Jake Delamare?"

Peter shook his head. "No, I can't say I've ever heard of him. Who is he?"

"Do you know somebody by the name of Minnie Wellings?"

Peter shifted uncomfortably in his seat.

I was starting to get a little worried. I hadn't had time to give Carl the please-be-tactful-for-once speech.

Carl sighed. "The thing is, Peter, Narel and I were wondering what brought you to this little town? A famous Cat Whisperer like you, coming to a quaint little town like this? It just doesn't make sense, if you don't mind me saying so. And what's even stranger, is that you happened to be in town right when your old nemesis, Stan Wellings, was murdered."

Peter gasped and reached into his bag.

CHAPTER 20

I thought Peter was going to pull out a gun, but to my enormous relief, he pulled out a white linen handkerchief and proceeded to dab at his brow.

"Carl!" I admonished him.

"You wanted to know just as much as I did, Narel," Carl said, rather put out. "You know you did!"

"I didn't murder Stan Wellings, if that's what the two of you are thinking," Peter said. "Sure, he did run off with my wife, but that was years ago, and we had an unhappy marriage, anyway."

"Go on," Carl said in a steely voice.

"I came to town to get away from all the attention. At first I was excited when my career took off, the television show, and everything, all the money. But I had a large social media platform."

"What's wrong with that?" Carl asked him.

"Do you know how many inboxes I get a day on Facebook?" Peter said. "Hundreds, and most of them are asking the very same questions that I have in my books.

People even say they can't find the information in my books. To give you an example, someone inboxed me and asked me how to litterbox train her cat. I told her which book that was in, but she said she couldn't find the information in that book. There was a whole chapter on it, a chapter called *Litterbox Training*. It might sound lame, but I've been hounded by the public, and I just want to go somewhere I'm not well-known. In fact, I decided to retire, but I just love what I do so much that I couldn't give it all up."

"That makes sense," I said, before I had really thought through whether or not it did.

Peter shot me a grateful look. "I shut down my Twitter and Instagram accounts. It's just all too much, and when I give people advice, they argue with me, or they don't take my advice, but sure enough, they come back and tell me they still have the same problem with their cats. If they had taken my advice in the first place, they wouldn't have a problem. It's all too much," he said again.

"So you don't know anyone called Jake Delamare?" Carl asked him again.

"No, I've never heard of him," Peter said. "I just wanted to find a small town, a small quiet country town where nothing ever happened, and where no one would notice me. I just wanted to be anonymous."

"If you wanted to be anonymous, you should have gone to a big city," I said. "I think a person's far less anonymous in a small country town. Everybody knows everyone else's business, and what they don't know, they make up."

Carl agreed. "And they know what you're doing before

you've even done it. And there are factions, too. You need to choose your sides wisely."

Peter looked confused, so Carl topped up his glass of bubbly.

Mongrel at that point noticed we had a visitor, and came out to sit on the spare chair opposite Peter.

"Aww, isn't that cute, he likes you," I said. "He only comes out of his basket to sit with people he likes."

"I don't know if it's a good idea to let cats sit on furniture," Peter said.

I waved a hand at him. "Okay then, feel free to tell him he can't sit there."

An unmistakable look of fear flashed across Peter's face. "I'm sure it's fine, in his case." He picked up his cat training bag and put it in front of him. I suppose it was a defensive gesture.

"You're perfectly safe," I said. "He only attacks people if there's rope around."

Peter held up his bandaged hands. "Yes, I noticed that."

Just then, Jake burst into the room from the back of the house.

He was wielding a large knife.

Carl screamed. I wanted to, but no sound would leave my mouth. Mongrel jumped from his chair and ran away. "Put your phones on the table where I can see them," Jake bellowed.

Carl and I did so, but Peter put his hand in his large bag. Jake was at his side in a flash and held up the knife in a threatening manner. "What's in your bag?" he snapped. He snatched the bag from Peter and looked in it. He pulled out Peter's phone, and then threw the bag back at

Peter. He tossed Peter's phone on the table with the other phones.

"So you figured it out, did you?" he said to me.

I didn't know whether to protest my innocence, or whether it would make him more angry if I did so.

"I've told the police," Carl said. "How did you get in?"

"I know how to get through a locked door. That back door is ancient." Jake reached for Carl's phone and then thumbed through it, while glancing up at us at intervals and brandishing the knife. "Oh, you did tell them," he said angrily. "Never mind, I'll take you all as hostages."

"Why would you need hostages?" I asked him. "The police aren't here yet. Just make a run for it."

"Minnie had nothing to do with it," he said. "It was me. I poisoned the chocolates."

"But you had an alibi," Carl said. I kicked him in the shins.

Jake appeared to be thinking that over. I was terrified, but I was running through it all in my mind, nevertheless. In this country, people are not allowed to profit from crime. That meant Minnie wouldn't get the inheritance if a jury convicted her of poisoning her father.

Jake seemed to have come up with a solution. "Okay then, you told the detective you saw me at Minnie's cottage. So what? If the cops can prove that we were seeing each other, that's one thing, but it's quite a jump to say that we both murdered her father."

"You're right," I said. "No one can prove anything, but it doesn't look good that you're in here waving a knife at us."

Jake sighed. "Shut your mouth, you skinny-fat woman. You know, you might be skinny, but you have no muscle tone." He said it as if it was the worst insult imaginable. "Okay then, we all know that Minnie and I killed Stan, so let's not beat about the bush. I came here to stop you telling the police, but you already did it. Now I just gotta figure out how to fix this situation."

"There *is* no way to fix this situation," I said.

Jake sneered at me. "Yes, there is. Minnie's on her way to get Mick. She's going to bring him here under some pretext, and then we'll make it look like a murder-suicide."

Peter spoke for the first time. "What do you mean?" he squeaked.

"Mick will shoot you all, and then shoot himself, at least that's how it will seem to the cops." His tone was menacing. He turned his attention to Carl. "But before that happens, I'll send the cops a message from your phone saying something to implicate Mick."

"You'll never get away with it." I regretted the words as soon as they were out of my mouth. I always thought it was lame when someone said it on TV, and now I thought it was even more lame.

"Shut your mouth. In fact, no one speaks, or you'll get it." He waved the knife at us to emphasise his point.

This couldn't be the end, not like this. I had survived a terrible car accident and had spent months in hospital, having surgery after surgery. Surely I couldn't die now at the hands of a nasty personal trainer. I only hoped that the police were on their way, but as soon as the thought occurred to me, I dismissed it. Rieker was likely to call, rather than simply turn up at my house.

I had been in this situation before, twice in fact, and on those occasions Mongrel had saved me. That gave me a glimmer of an idea, but I found it hard to concentrate because I was in fear for my life.

"I suppose it's good that you're going to shoot us and not hang us," I said, risking speaking after I had been told not to. "My cat hates rope." I gave Peter a significant look, but unfortunately, he didn't seem to catch on.

"My cat hates rope," I said again.

"I told you to shut up," Jake snapped. He went to the window and moved the curtain a little.

"Peter, Jake might need some rope," I said. "Do you have any?"

Peter's eyebrows shot up, and he nodded slightly.

My speaking clearly annoyed Jake, because he stormed back over to me, his knife in hand. Peter reached in his bag and pulled out a length of rope which he flung at Jake. Jake had good reflexes, because he spun around and caught it. "What the?" Those were the only words he got out.

The next thing I knew, he was on his back, screaming. "Quick, get the knife, Carl," I said.

Carl shook his head. "I'm not going anywhere near that cat."

I stepped over to Jake and kicked the knife away.

"Carl, call the police now," I said.

"And an ambulance," Peter said in a weak voice. I looked up to see he had his hands firmly clamped over his eyes. I couldn't blame him. The piece of rope he had thrown at Jake was sizeable.

"Can you call your cat off?" Peter added, peeking between his fingers.

"I don't know how to, but you're the cat expert."

Peter shut his eyes again.

Detective Clyde and Detective Rieker arrived at the same time as the ambulance. Jake was still screaming when they took him away.

"So, your cat has done it again, Miss Myers," Clyde said. "He'll probably get a medal for that."

"Really?" I asked with delight.

"No." Clyde looked at me as though I were mad.

Rieker and Carl were talking in a corner. Peter The Purr-suader was sitting on the sofa, his hands still firmly over his eyes. "Peter was the one who saved us all," I said. "He was the one who threw the rope at Jake."

Peter managed a weak smile, but Clyde did not seem impressed. "We have rounded up Minnie," he said. "She wasn't too happy when we told her that Jake had confessed to everything."

"I bet she wasn't," I said. I looked past him to see a figure standing in the doorway. "Tom, what are you doing here?"

"I heard police and ambulance sirens, and I thought of you."

I didn't quite know how to take that, so I just smiled and nodded. "It was Jake," I told him. "Jake and Minnie were in it together."

Peter finally managed to speak. "Jake came here to kill us all," he said.

Tom's face went white. He crossed the room in five quick strides and took me into his arms.

CHAPTER 21

The following night, Carl and I threw a party for Mongrel. Tom and Peter The Purr-suader were there, as was Detective Rieker. We had invited Detective Clyde, but he had declined. He had, however, sent along a packet of treats for Mongrel. Maybe that guy wasn't so bad, after all.

I had spent the day in bed, with a hot water bottle and plenty of liniment. I had received several voicemail messages from the horrible reporter, Graham Gibson, wanting to interview me over my celebrity cat, as he put it.

Mongrel was sitting on his own chair in the living room looking quite pleased with himself. Everyone was giving him a wide berth, especially when someone threw him a treat and he devoured it with his usual ferocity.

"You know, Narel, that was a close call," Carl said.

"*Another* close call," Rieker added. "I don't know how you two manage to attract so much trouble."

"We don't attract it," I protested. "It just kind of finds us."

"I suppose that's what Rieker means," Carl said, and Rieker shot him a warm smile.

I was sitting on the sofa. Tom was sitting next to me with his arm around me protectively. I quite liked that. "I really don't like you being involved in murders," Tom said, giving my shoulders a little squeeze.

"Trust me, I don't like it either," I said.

"Oh well, it will probably never happen again," Tom said, although Carl and I exchanged glances.

"Have you ever read that famous book on morphic resonance?" Carl asked Tom, ignoring my warning glares.

"I've never heard of it," Peter said.

"It means if something happens once, it will draw the same kind of thing to it. That's probably not a very good explanation, but that's basically it in a nutshell. The theory goes that a pattern of events can facilitate occurrences of similar events."

Peter frowned. "Does that mean you and Narel are likely to be involved in further murders?"

"Of course not!" I said, shooting Carl another warning glance. I decided to change the subject. "Peter, do you still want to work on Mongrel to help him with his aggression problems?"

A look of horror briefly flickered over Peter's face. "No, I don't think so." That was all he said—he didn't give any further reason. I suppose seeing what Mongrel did to Jake was reason enough.

"The doctors say Jake will be out of intensive care in a few days," Rieker offered helpfully.

We all nodded. There was really nothing to say to that, although Mongrel purred.

"What's that fearsome sound?" Rieker asked in alarm, looking around him.

"That's just Mongrel purring," I said.

Rieker frowned. "Are you sure? It sounds like thunder, or an earthquake."

I shook my head. "He purrs like that when he's very happy."

"That means he feels secure," Peter said. "You have done a good job with him, Narel."

Rieker looked at him in disbelief. "Haven't you seen what that cat does to people?"

Peter held up his bandaged hands by way of response. "Rescue cats often have Post Traumatic Stress Disorder," he told him. "Mongrel only reacts that way to rope. If there is no rope around, then he's a very happy, nice cat."

"I think that's probably something of an exaggeration," Rieker said with a laugh.

Mongrel's purring grew louder, so much so, that it shook his chair. I was glad to see that he had come a long way. Now he was sitting in a room with several people and he wasn't at all afraid.

I felt like purring, too. It was likely the feeling of euphoria that came after facing a traumatic event, and surviving. And I had my good friends around me, Carl, my best friend, and Tom, my crush. Even Mongrel, my rescue cat, had my back.

Life was pretty good.

NEXT BOOK IN THIS SERIES

CHOCOLATE TO DIE FOR (COCOA NAREL CHOCOLATE SHOP MYSTERIES BOOK 4)

Narel calls a plumber to fix the outdoor toilet behind her chocolate shop. Her best friend, Carl, finds the plumber dead. At first the police think he died from a redback spider bite, but tests reveal otherwise.

As cracks begin to form in the case, the police uncover nasty emails between Carl and the victim. As Narel chews on the problem, she finds that the plumber's customers had nothing sweet to say about him.

What happens when Narel uncovers Carl's secret that he has been keeping tightly wrapped?

Can Narel solve the murder before the situation becomes too sticky?

ALSO BY MORGANA BEST

Live and Let Diet (The Australian Amateur Sleuth Book 1)

Sybil Potts moves to Little Tatterford, a small town in the middle of nowhere in Australia, seeking to find peace and quiet after the upheaval of her divorce.

Although the town is sleepy and nothing has ever happened, her arrival coincides with a murder in the property adjacent to her cottage. Sybil soon finds she is at odds with the attractive Blake Wessley, the exasperated police officer who is trying to solve the murder.

After Sibyl narrowly misses becoming the next victim, she turns her attention to the suspects. Is it the English gentleman, Mr. Buttons, who serves everyone tea and cucumber sandwiches, or her landlord, Cressida Upthorpe, who is convinced that her fat cat, Lord Farringdon, speaks to her? Or is it someone else entirely?

Miss Spelled (The Kitchen Witch Book 1)

Amelia Spelled has had a bad week. Her boyfriend dumps her when she inadvertently gives him food poisoning; her workplace, a telecommunications centre, fires all their staff as they are outsourcing offshore, and she is evicted due to smoke damage resulting from her failed attempts at baking. Amelia thinks her luck has changed when she inherits her aunt's store and beautiful Victorian house.

Yet has Amelia jumped out of the frying pan into the fire? The store is a cake store, and her aunt was a witch. To add to the mix, the house has secrets all of its own.

When a man is murdered in the cake store, will Amelia be able to cook up a way to solve the crime? Or will her spells prove as bad as her baking?

A Ghost of a Chance (Witch Woods Funeral Home Book 1)

Nobody knows that Laurel Bay can see and talk to ghosts. When she inherits a funeral home, she is forced to return from the city to the small town of Witch Woods to breathe life into the business. It is a grave responsibility, but Laurel is determined that this will be no dead-end job.

There she has to contend with her manipulative and overly religious mother, more than one ghost, and a secretive but handsome accountant.

When the murder of a local woman in the funeral home strangles the finances, can Laurel solve the murder?

Or will this be the death of her business?

Note: This book is humorously irreverent in places, so please read only if you won't be offended.

Christmas Spirit (The Middle-aged Ghost Whisper Book 1)

Prudence Wallflower tours the country, making live appearances. She connects people with loved ones who have passed on. However, her reputation as a clairvoyant medium is failing, and even Prudence has begun to doubt herself. She has never seen a ghost, but receives impressions from the dead. This all changes when the ghost of a detective appears to her and demands her help to solve a murder. Prudence finds herself out of her depth, and to make matters worse, she is more attracted to this ghost than any man she has ever met.

SERIES BY MORGANA BEST

Vampires and Wine (A fun, quirky cozy mystery series - no fangs involved!)

1) Witches' Brew - *Now on Audio!*

2) Witches' Secrets - *Now on Audio!*

3) Witches' Charms

4) Witches Spells

The Kitchen Witch

1) **Miss Spelled** - *Now on Audio!*

2) Dizzy Spells - *Now on Audio!*

3) Sit for a Spell - *Now on Audio!*

4) Spelling Mistake - *Now on Audio!*

5) Ex-Spelled - *Now on Audio!*

6) The Halloween Spell

7) Spellcheck

8) The Halloween Love Spell

9) Spell It Out

The Middle-aged Ghost Whisperer

1) **Christmas Spirit** - *Now on Audio!*

2) Ghost Hunter

3) There Must be a Happy Medium

Witch Woods Funeral Home

1) **A Ghost of a Chance**- *Now on Audio!*

2) Nothing to Ghost About - *Now on Audio!*

3) Make the Ghost of It

4) Ghost Stories

5) Ghost Blusters

And Morgana's *non-Witch* Cosy mysteries:

Cocoa Narel Chocolate Shop Mysteries

1) Sweet Revenge

2) The Sugar Hit

3) Murder Sweetly Served

4) Chocolate to Die For

The Australian Amateur Sleuth

1) Live and Let Diet

2) Natural-Born Grillers

3) Dye Hard

4) The Prawn Identity

5) Any Given Sundae

6) The Last Mango in Paris

AUDIO. All Morgana's books are currently being narrated for Audio.

ABOUT MORGANA BEST

Best selling Aussie author, Morgana Best, grew up leaving Tim Tams for the fairies at the bottom of her garden. Now she lives with a half-blind Chocolate Labrador who happily walks into doors, a rescue Dingo who steals zucchinis from the veggie patch, and a cat with no time for nonsense. A former college professor, Morgana enjoys big bowls of pasta, not working out, and visiting the local lighthouse, where she tries to spot the white humpback whale.

www.morganabest.com

64703626R00122

Made in the USA
Lexington, KY
17 June 2017